# "A Diamond Engagement Ring?" Randi Stared At The Gold-Banded Gem Manuel Had Given Her. What Was He Telling Her?

"Not a diamond." He narrowed his eyes. "A fake ring, for a fake engagement."

A scarlet flush of embarrassment rushed up her throat and covered her face. Of course. Despite the kiss they'd shared last night, this was just part of his job.

But it could also be a chance to keep Manuel and the child on the ranch. Close by her. Maybe, with a little more time, she could find out for once in her life what having a man and a family of her own would be like—even if it was only a temporary situation.

At the thought, an ache of longing thudded in her heart, so strong it nearly knocked her down.

*Dear God.* Could she really pull this off—and not be destroyed in the process...?

Dear Reader,

Dog days of summer got you down? Chill out and relax with six brand-new love stories from Silhouette Desire!

August's MAN OF THE MONTH is the first book in the exciting family-based saga BECKETT'S FORTUNE by Dixie Browning. *Beckett's Cinderella* features a hero honor-bound to repay a generations-old debt and a poor-but-proud heroine leery of love and money she can't believe is offered unconditionally. *His E-Mail Order Wife* by Kristi Gold, in which matchmaking relatives use the Internet to find a high-powered exec a bride, is the latest title in the powerful DYNASTIES: THE CONNELLYS series.

A daughter seeking revenge discovers love instead in *Falling for the Enemy* by Shawna Delacorte. Then, in *Millionaire Cop & Mom-To-Be* by Charlotte Hughes, a jilted, pregnant bride is rescued by her childhood sweetheart.

Passion flares between a family-minded rancher and a marriage-shy divorcée in Kathie DeNosky's *Cowboy Boss*. And a pretend marriage leads to undeniable passion in *Desperado Dad* by Linda Conrad.

So find some shade, grab a cold one…and read all six passionate, powerful and provocative new love stories from Silhouette Desire this month.

Enjoy!

*Joan Marlow Golan*

Joan Marlow Golan
Senior Editor, Silhouette Desire

Please address questions and book requests to:
Silhouette Reader Service
U.S.: 3010 Walden Ave., P.O. Box 1325, Buffalo, NY 14269
Canadian: P.O. Box 609, Fort Erie, Ont. L2A 5X3

# Desperado Dad
## LINDA CONRAD

Published by Silhouette Books
**America's Publisher of Contemporary Romance**

SILHOUETTE BOOKS

ISBN 0-373-76458-8

DESPERADO DAD

Copyright © 2002 by Linda Lucas Sankpill

Visit Silhouette at www.eHarlequin.com

**Printed in U.S.A.**

**Books by Linda Conrad**

Silhouette Desire

*The Cowboy's Baby Surprise* #1446
*Desperado Dad* #1458

# LINDA CONRAD

was born in Brazil to a commercial pilot dad and a mother whose first gift was a passion for stories. She was raised in South Florida and has been a dreamer and a storyteller for as long as she can remember. Linda claims her earliest memories are of sitting in her mother's lap listening to a beloved storybook or searching through the picture books in the library to find that special one.

When Linda met and married her own dream-come-true hero, he fostered another of her other inherited vices—being a vagabond. They moved to seven different states in seven years, finally becoming enchanted with and settling down in the Rio Grande Valley of Texas.

Reality anchored Linda to their Texas home long enough to raise a daughter and become a stockbroker and certified financial planner. Her whole world suddenly changed when her widowed mother suffered a disabling stroke and Linda spent a year as her caretaker. Before her mother's second and fatal stroke, she begged Linda to go back to her dreams—to finally tell the stories buried within her heart.

Linda's hobbies are reading, growing roses and experiencing new things. However, her real passion is "passion"—reading about it, writing about it and living it. She believes that true passion and intensity for life and love are seductive—they consume the soul and make life's trials and tribulations worth all the effort.

"I am extremely grateful that today I can live my dreams by being able to share the passionate stories and lovable characters that have lived deep within me for so long," Linda declares.

Linda loves to hear from her readers and invites them to visit her Web site at http://www.lindaconrad.com.

To both my darling husband and sister, because Manny's story is your favorite. To Dana Rae Link, because you started all this years ago. And especially for Emily, because I couldn't do any of them without you.

# One

Manny Sanchez decided the pounding rain did have one advantage—it helped to hide his stealthy nighttime chase. He rode his Harley through the bitter, biting and brutal sleet, torn between cursing the storm and being grateful for the added cover.

In the next instant the minivan he'd been following slowed. When its brake lights glowed red, memories of devastating car wrecks flashed before his eyes. He'd seen plenty of twisted metal in his thirty-four years, and a flashback of his own agony clutched at his chest.

Damn. Not this time. A baby boy was riding inside that van. Life had always been cruel as far as Manny was concerned, but the baby's short, tragic life simply must not end this way. Manny couldn't let that happen—not again.

Through his rain-distorted visor, he watched horrified as the minivan carrying the *coyote* and his cargo came to a low-water bridge. They hit a patch of icy highway and slid sideways. Manny winced.

*¡Ay, Dios mio!* No one will get out alive!

Suddenly his bike hit another frozen spot and he lost control. He cut the power, laying the bike down into the gravel covering the side of the road. His leather-clad, left shoulder took the entire brunt of the roadway collision, but a combination of adrenaline and freezing cold numbed him to the effects he knew were sure to follow.

Luckily the bike slid across the asphalt, scattering sparks and landing in a field, while he sprawled down the gravel in the other direction. His heavy jeans protected him from the rocks and wet pavement.

When his forward momentum finally eased, he jumped to his feet, relieved he was still able to walk. But there wasn't time to check for broken bones or bleeding. He ripped off his helmet, flung it aside and ran toward the bridge.

In terrifying slow motion, Manny watched the minivan lose contact with the asphalt as it hit the rushing water. Within the space of a heartbeat, the boxy little vehicle turned on its side and was swept into the furious torrent.

A breath hitched in his throat as he stood paralyzed, seeing the scene unfold before him. Shock and a fleeting sense of sorrow and guilt overtook him. Why hadn't he found a way to end this assignment earlier today—or yesterday? Or, hell, last week before things had gotten so out of hand?

He clearly heard the eerie shriek of twisting metal over the sounds of howling water as torrents assaulted the minivan with a devastating rampage. The incessant beating of the rain competed with the hammering of his heart.

Without a moment for recriminations and once again burying his emotions, he reacted to the tragedy the way he'd been trained—don't hesitate, act.

Just then the minivan snagged itself on a pile of debris clogged against willows at the side of the raging river. It was all the advantage Manny would get, and he ran toward the van before it broke loose and dashed farther downstream.

By the time he reached the car, lying precariously driver's side down, he'd made an assessment of what he could do, and what the chances were that anyone had survived. The van was submerged a good three feet deep, and the black water still rose against it. Since the roof was all he could see from the bank, he couldn't be sure, but...

Manny scrambled up the hood and scaled the front window, ignoring the pain in his shoulder. Slick and slippery, the van rocked gently as the cascading water tore at it, making any assent more than hazardous.

After too many precious minutes, he made it to the passenger side and knelt, yanking on the front passenger door. It took a supreme effort, but the door finally opened, revealing the murky interior.

"Hey, can you hear me?" he shouted.

He bent closer and realized no one sat in the passenger seat. For a second the silence from inside was so complete he wondered if the worst had already happened.

He began lowering himself into the front toward the spot where a driver should be, when a child's cry pulled him up short. The baby was still alive! But Manny couldn't see him for all the darkness and water.

With another small whimper from the back seat, Manny quickly reached into the murky water where the driver should be and found—nothing. The smuggler that had been driving must have been thrown out as the van went over.

As fast as he could, Manny dragged himself out of the van and wrestled with the sliding back door. The more he pulled the worse his shoulder throbbed.

The door eventually gave way to his efforts. Manny saw the kid, still strapped in his child-carrier and hanging sideways as the water rose to meet him.

*Please don't let him die.*

Manny reached for the carrier's seat belt and gave it a jerk. Nothing happened. The damn thing was stuck, so Manny lowered himself into the car, sliding past the suddenly too-quiet child and landing in the freezing water.

Standing upright in the back, waist deep, with his feet resting on the car's left side window, he reached into his jeans pocket for his knife. As Manny's fingers grasped the pocket knife, a small hand reached out to touch his face.

"Hi, baby, are you hurting?" He tried to keep the tension from his voice. "I'll have you out of here in a minute."

The dark-haired child, dressed in nothing but a red sweater and diaper, started to sob. It wasn't a loud cry, but a soft, heart-wrenching sound that tore into Manny's soul.

"Pa...ba?" The baby patted Manny's face and reached grasping fingers toward his jacket.

"I'm not your papa, *hijo,* but there's no need to be afraid. I won't let anything else happen to you."

A flash of memory passed through Manny's mind, reminding him that this little one had already lost his father and his mother forever. That was enough. Manny vowed to keep him safe from now on—no matter what it took, and no matter who didn't care for the idea.

With more effort than Manny's shoulder should handle, the seat belt finally gave way to his sharp blade. The baby grabbed him around the neck and hung on desperately.

Manny flipped the blade closed and jammed it back into his pocket while he experienced the closest thing to sheer panic he'd ever felt. How in the world was he going to lift himself and the boy out of the back seat and onto the car's side with this injured shoulder?

"Hand the baby to me."

"What the...?" The woman's voice coming from above startled the hell out of him.

When he looked up, all he could make out were long slender arms reaching down into the open doorway. Where had she come from? Had she been inside the van and gotten out by herself? Impossible. But then where... and how...?

"Hurry up. I don't think we've got much time." The woman's demand shocked him into movement. He lifted the baby up with his good arm. The seemingly disembodied arms from above grabbed hold of the boy securely.

The baby gasped and tightened his grip on Manny and wailed.

"Easy, sweetheart, I've got you." The woman's voice turned soft and pleading.

Manny pried the boy's arms from his neck as gently as he possibly could. Meanwhile the woman made soothing noises, pulling the baby upward. Once they had disappeared from view, Manny used his good arm and his legs to drag himself up and out of the car.

When he found a steady perch on the car's side, he looked over to the woman, who had the little boy wrapped securely in her arms. She looked hesitantly over the slippery roof to the ground just beyond reach.

The rain still pulsated down on them, making every movement difficult. Manny made a quick decision. He slid down the roof and managed to find a fairly solid foothold on top of wet debris and clogged tree branches.

He reached his good arm up toward the woman and child. "Hand him back to me, then slide down. I'll steady you."

She hesitated. "Your arm's hurt. Can you hold him?"

"It's nothing. Just a bruised shoulder."

She looked unsure but lowered the baby to him. The boy grabbed a handful of black leather jacket and held on in a death grip. Meanwhile the mysterious woman eased herself down the roof while Manny steadied her with his body.

Within seconds they were standing on muddy ground.

"Is there anyone else in there?" she shouted over the roar of the wind and water.

Manny shook his head.

She turned to the car and then swirled back with an undecided glance. For the first time, Manny noticed what their mysterious savior looked like: about half a foot shorter than his six feet, her long soggy hair hung down her back in wet strands. She wore a neon yellow slicker that looked three sizes too big and hung on her slender frame, making her appear younger than the midtwenties he guessed she must be.

It was her eyes that really grabbed him, though. Wide with questions, Manny couldn't tell exactly what color they were in the blackness of the night surrounding them. Full of all the emotions that he knew swirled inside her, those eyes made her look sweet and strong, and right this minute, downright scared.

He spent one precious second considering the slim chance that the baby-stealing minivan driver still lived. It seemed like a tough ending for the man who'd obviously panicked back in Del Rio and had appeared to be headed straight for his boss. Mother Nature hadn't read him his rights.

In all the years Manny had been undercover chasing these baby smugglers for Operation Rock-a-Bye, he'd never followed any of them so far from the border. Usually the actual kidnapping happened in Mexico or in Europe and then was funneled through Mexico. And it was in the big, Texas cities where most of the baby selling took place. The thought of murderers and scum living in a safe, small town troubled him.

It would be impossible to find the body tonight, so he buried his uneasiness. Right now the living needed tending.

With no hesitation he gathered the woman up next to him and forced his bad shoulder to cradle her, while he tightened his grip on the baby with his good arm. "We need to get out of the rain. Now."

"My...my truck."

He dragged her toward the roadway. They hadn't gone more than a few feet when the raging water finally tore the minivan loose and pummeled it farther down the river.

The sickening sounds of scraping metal against rock forced Manny into action. He picked up their pace and moved the little band of survivors up the incline at the riverbank.

Farther up the hill, parked in the middle of the pavement, Manny saw what had to be the woman's truck. A fifteen-year-old, four-wheel-drive Suburban sat idling with its lights on.

"Are you okay to drive?" he asked.

She nodded and swung into the front seat. Scooting over to open the passenger door for Manny and the baby, she took the boy while Manny climbed into the truck and, closing the door behind him, gathered the child back into his arms.

Manny unzipped his jacket, put the baby on his chest and zipped the jacket back up over both of them, keeping the baby secure and a little warmer. If this truck wrecked on the icy roads, the baby's position against him might be dangerous, but without Manny's body heat the little boy was sure to go into shock.

He looked over to the woman and noticed she'd belted herself in, but her hands shook so badly he was afraid she'd never keep hold of the wheel. Manny reached across the baby and jacked up the heater's fan.

"You sure you can drive?"

"Ye-e-e-s-s," she stuttered. "The way the water's rising, we're about to be cut off by two flooding rivers. Happens every time things get this bad. My ranch is just a ways up the road. It's the only possible chance we've got."

Jamming the truck into Reverse, she eased it around on the asphalt and slowly drove away from the river.

He suddenly realized he didn't know her name, or why she'd been there to help them. "I need to thank you for coming to our rescue. It was a very brave but foolhardy thing to do." She kept her attention on the slick road, continuing to stare out the windshield.

"I'm Manny Sanchez. And you are…"

"Randi."

"Excuse me?"

"That's my name. I'm Randi Cullen. And I live on the Running C ranch."

The Running C? Son of a gun, if that wasn't the name he'd overheard the smugglers discussing at the café in Del Rio. Was this woman involved with them? All of a sudden it occurred to him that their savior might really be the suspect he'd been seeking. But the only way to find out would be to keep a sharp eye on her.

Manny quickly decided he'd better keep her close—whatever that took and any way he could.

Randi tightened her grip on the steering wheel and slanted a glance at the dark and intimidating man who was scrutinizing her from the passenger seat. The energy emanating from him hummed with tension. Dear Lord, he terrified—and excited—her.

She couldn't figure out what had possessed her to climb up on that minivan the way she had. There hadn't been time to consider the ramifications, just like now, when there was no choice but to take this menacing man and his child into her home.

After she'd stopped at the bridge and heard the baby's cry, all sense of personal danger had deserted her. She could still feel the rush of bravado, sitting here in the front seat with a total stranger. She'd never done anything like this in her entire life. Just thinking about it made her tremble.

Nevertheless, Randi felt more alive in the past half hour than she had in years. Bringing this man home might be a very dangerous thing to do, but she didn't care. Somehow she felt sure he would be trustworthy. He had an aura about him that reminded her of her old friend, the deputy sheriff.

The stranger had been traveling with his own child. How bad could he be? And what's more, he and his baby needed help, and she'd been able to do something about it. That frustrating feeling of being unable to do anything to help, the one emotion she'd been so familiar with over the past few years, was slowly washing away as the minutes went by.

"That's a kind of unusual name for a woman, isn't it?" he asked.

"Randi? It was my grandmother's nickname." At his seemingly confused look, she explained, "Short for Miranda…?"

"I wasn't questioning it. I think Randi is a beautiful name."

She could feel the flush stealing over her face. Glancing over at him, she found a smirk of amusement. The smile lit up his entire face, making him the most magnetic man she'd ever laid eyes on.

Oh, not handsome in the standard movie star way, his jaw was too sharp and his nose too long and broad for that. But he was intense, dark and a little rough around the edges, as if a thin veneer of civilized behavior covered a raging beast inside. And he was big—broad. Her breathing faltered when she realized how much of the front seat he really occupied.

"My mother named me," she managed shakily.

"Well, Randi." He repeated her name with emphasis. "Far be it from me to question good fortune, but what the heck were you doing out here in this deluge?"

"I…" She had to swallow down the lump in her throat and put aside her jitters. "I was on my way home from town. When I heard about the storm, I stopped at the grocery store after work. That's why I'm late." She was babbling and tried to slow down.

She took a deep breath and inhaled the scent of wet leather, sweat and musky man. An odd sensation, one she couldn't name and had never felt before, coiled inside her.

Randi found herself sneaking a peek at his ring finger.

"I saw a car's headlights turn at the creek road," she began. "Everyone who lives around here knows not to take a low-water bridge road in a storm, so I figured it must be strangers. I knew there'd be trouble."

Empty. No rings on his hands at all. But that didn't mean much in these modern times. And there *was* the matter of his baby.

Randi suddenly remembered the child. When she turned her head to check on him, she was surprised to see the shaggy, black-haired desperado of a man gently patting the back of the baby who lay quietly on his chest.

"We can't make it to the hospital before the highway is flooded out. Is the baby going to be all right? Will you manage?"

"I guess we'll find out," he mumbled.

"What's the baby's name?"

"Uh, I don't…Ricardo…Ricky," he finally stammered.

Maybe Manny was as flustered by the circumstances as she was? Nope. Not the gritty and unswerving male who'd helped her and the baby off the slick minivan in the middle of the storm.

"And I think he's going to be fine. He stopped shivering a few minutes ago." Manny glanced down at the top of the toddler's head, then peered out the window into the dark night. "I would like to get him dried off, though."

"Right. Looks like we beat the water. We're almost there." As a matter of fact, at that moment the rusty gate bearing the Running C brand came into view.

Randi threw the car into Park and jumped out to open

the gate—which turned out to be not an easy task with all the mud flowing across the gravel road.

She groaned internally at the thought of how rutted and pocked her road would be after the rain. And she didn't have enough money to have it graded this time, either.

Gritting her teeth with frustration, Randi shoved at the heavy gate and then plowed her way back to the truck. The darn thing could just stay open. She didn't care. No way was she getting out of the truck again to close it in this downpour.

Back in the driver's seat, Randi could feel icy water dripping on her neck. The droplets didn't stop there, but ran under her collar and slithered down her back. She started to shiver involuntarily but pressed her lips together and kept driving.

Only another half a mile to go.

It seemed like an hour's drive, but actually within a few minutes she pulled up in the yard. Ignoring her usual parking spot under the tree, Randi drove as close to the back porch as she could manage.

"This is it. Let me put on a light and then I'll come back out and help with the baby." She ducked her head as she opened the truck door against the heavy rain and wind.

Just inside the door to the house, Manny stomped his boots and tried to shake the bulk of the water from his body, without much luck. He was soaked clean through.

When Randi had turned on the porch light, he'd caught a glimpse of her ranch house through the pouring rain. It hadn't made much of an impression. From what Manny could see, the porch stairs leaned precariously to one side and the back door could obviously stand a new coat of paint.

Now he found himself in an old-fashioned mud room, with thirty-year-old linoleum on the floor and yellowing wallpaper on the walls. He clutched the baby to his chest, not wanting him to get a chill. Manny could still see his breath in the air even though they were inside the house.

"That's all of it." Randi came back through the door, carrying two bags full of groceries. "Come into the kitchen, while I light the stove. It'll only take a few minutes to warm up."

She dragged off her slicker, shaking it as she hung it on a peg. Leading the way through the mud room and into the kitchen, she turned on lights as she went.

Without the raincoat, she looked like a drowned rat. Well, actually, more like a drowned mouse. Thin and pale, her long, straight hair had almost dried, and he noticed only that it was the color of dishwater. She had on a dark pants outfit that appeared to be permanently wrinkled and stained by the rain.

The only memorable things about her were her eyes. In the light he saw their magical color. Hazel, he supposed they'd call them on a rap sheet. But one minute they were pale green ringed by steel blue, the next minute they were a deep gold with bronze flecks. The vulnerability he'd found within them haunted him more than the interesting colors.

Suddenly conscious of what a wet mess he was making, Manny stepped onto one of the braided rugs covering the wooden plank floor. Holding the baby against his shoulder, he silently apologized to the child for having to make up a name and for continuing to drag him

along during an investigation. He stayed at the far end
of the room and let his eyes adjust to the dim light.

He slowly focused, staring into the wide-open area
that served as a kitchen and looked as if it had been
furnished in the forties. His gaze took in all the details
of the room: the propane-powered icebox with the fan
on top, the floor-to-ceiling, free-standing breakfront,
used as a pantry, and the two-foot thick, butcher block
table in the middle of the room.

The out-of-date feel to the place reminded him of
Mexico. Everything here was well-worn but also well
cared for and spotless.

Randi busied herself shoving chopped wood into a
cast-iron stove, the kind that had become very trendy in
some areas of the West. Manny seriously doubted if
she'd bought the thing to be fashionable. It looked ancient, but usable.

She lit the fire and fiddled with a damper. "It won't
be long now." Her gaze caught his and flicked away.
"Let me get some towels and a blanket for your baby."

When she disappeared down a hall, Manny was
shocked to realize he'd been studying her with more than
just the professional eye of an undercover special agent.
He found he'd been sidetracked once again by those
amazing hazel-green eyes.

As she spoke, she'd looked like a timid fawn. Her
skin was pearly with a dash of freckles across the nose.
Only average height and a little too thin, as well, he
thought. But her hips did curve rather seductively in the
dressy slacks she wore.

All in all there wasn't a reason in the world for the
lick of desire he'd felt when their gazes met. He'd most
assuredly felt it, though. And was, in fact, still trying to
recover from the jolt.

Randi came back into the room with an armful of linens. "Here, let me have Ricky. You get out of that jacket and start drying off."

After she set the pile of towels and blankets on the counter, he handed her the little boy and peeled off his soggy leather jacket. Manny was surprised to find the room considerably warmer than it had been just a few minutes earlier. He didn't bother trying to figure out whether the warmth was related to the temperature or came from the nearness of the woman.

He took a deep breath and smelled a heady combination of mesquite smoke, dried herbs and tangy oranges. Reaching to pull off his boots, he had the weird sensation of being here before, of feeling at home. Maybe it was because the place felt like a safe haven, reminding him of his grandmother's house in Mexico.

Manny stood transfixed, with a water-filled boot in each hand, watching as Randi undressed the baby and towel dried his hair. She was easy with Ricky, warm and motherly, and she turned Manny's senses to mush.

Son of a gun. This innocent couldn't possibly be involved with the baby smugglers. It wouldn't be fair.

For the first time since he'd taken the oath, he hated what he did for a living. Hated having to pretend to be something he wasn't. Hated having decent people be afraid of him.

But the truth was, when push came to shove, if Randi was involved with the smuggling ring, he'd do his job and take her down. The ruthless, international baby snatchers deserved no mercy. He just had to pray this guileless young woman was exactly as she seemed.

As soon as humanly possible, Manny needed to banish his emotions once more and get out of her house and her life—with his libido and his soul safely intact.

# Two

"The phone's on the wall behind you." The sound of Randi's voice broke into Manny's daydream.

"Can you dial the operator and ask to speak to the sheriff's office?" She kept a hand on Ricky while speaking to Manny over her shoulder. "I think we should report your wreck and see what needs to be done."

Before they contacted any sheriff, Manny needed to contact his boss at Operation Rock-a-Bye. Without saying a word to Randi, he shoved his wet jacket and boots into the washroom and picked up the phone. "The line's dead."

"Oh, dear. The storm must be worse. That means the electricity will be next." She wrapped the lethargic baby in a heavy blanket and handed him over to Manny. "We'd better get a move on. There's a shower stall off the mud room. You and the baby get under the warm water. I'll start a fire in the front room."

When she turned to move away from him, Manny clamped a hand over her arm. Her skin was ice-cold.

"Is there anyone else in the house? Anyone you're expecting?"

She shook her head and jerked on her arm, but he didn't release her. Not just yet. "You need to warm up as much as we do. You're shivering. You take the baby into the shower. I'll start the fire."

"No...no." She eased her arm away from his grasp, and he released her reluctantly. "I know where everything is. You don't. I'll light some kerosene lanterns just in case. And I'm pretty sure there's a trunk in the attic with some baby things—maybe even clothes that'll fit you."

She tilted her head, letting her gaze travel up his full length, making him feel naked and taking him in a direction he didn't want to go.

"Well, maybe at least something that'll do in an emergency." With that pronouncement, she swiveled on the balls of her feet and headed to the door. "I'll get changed while I'm upstairs. I'll be okay." She turned her head to look in his direction. "Everything will be okay."

"Right," he muttered as she disappeared. "Everything's going to be just swell."

Randi almost made it back downstairs before the power went out. Almost. Instead, she wasted time speculating about the dangerous-looking man and child she'd taken into her home.

The lights blinked once, then plunged the house into a familiar darkness. Without missing a step, she reached for the candle and some matches she'd stashed in the attic for emergencies. Lately one problem or another caused a power outage every month, and she simply didn't have the money to buy a new generator.

Lighting the candle and inching her way to the darkened stairs, Randi's mind went back to the broad-shouldered man who'd been dressed head to toe in black. When he'd stepped into her kitchen and taken off the leather jacket, she'd caught a glimpse of rippled muscles under his inky-colored T-shirt and jeans.

The man emanated power and excitement. Never in her life had she seen so much macho packed into one person. He was charming and terribly good-looking, in a sexy sort of way. But all that was just window dressing.

He made the words *take charge, dynamo,* and *daring* seem inadequate. Did his honey-brown eyes really absorb her every thought, word and deed, especially when she hadn't said or done anything at all? Did he really manage to discover her wishes and desires without a word? Even his body appeared to vibrate with static energy as he stood perfectly still.

No, Manny Sanchez was nothing like any of the men she'd ever known. Randi had read about such heroes in novels, had seen a couple in movies when she was a girl. She'd even dreamed about them from time to time, but the idea of really meeting one this dynamic had never crossed her mind. And now she'd taken him into her house.

A shiver rippled along her spine as she crept down the stairs. If it hadn't been an emergency situation, and if it hadn't been for the baby...

The thought of Ricky made Randi hasten her steps. Precariously balanced, with a basket of clothes in one hand and a candle in the other, she worried about the child. That little one didn't seem well to her, his eyes were glazed and his cry weak. She fervently hoped that with some warmth and dry clothes he might be okay.

When she crept into her front room, she found a massive hulk huddled by the fire. Manny must have found another blanket. This one totally covered him like a tent as he kept his back to her and faced the warmth of the hearth.

Randi accidentally stepped on a creaky floor board and jumped nearly a foot at the noise.

"Did you get a shower before the power went out?" Manny asked. Wincing at the pain from his tender shoulder, he shifted the baby against his chest before turning. He'd known by her light footsteps that he'd be facing the young woman who'd given them shelter.

She'd changed into well-worn jeans and a frayed, navy sweatshirt with a Texas Aggie logo. The sweatshirt was thin with age, and he couldn't help but notice the way her nipples beaded against it in the cold.

With her wet hair tied up in a towel, she looked so fragile his first impulse was to gather her up in his arms and set her on a shelf somewhere. In his current state of undress that would be more than stupid on his part, even if she would allow it.

Randi set down the basket she'd been carrying by the hearth. "No, no time for a shower. But I'm fairly dry and the fire will warm me up fast enough." She pulled a kerosene lamp from the mantel and lit it before blowing out her candle. "Did you find everything you needed?"

He suppressed a chuckle. "I didn't even bother looking. I did find the clothesline in the mud room and hung our soggy stuff over it, but Ricky needs a few things you probably don't have."

She dug into the basket and pulled out a square white cloth. "Like this, you mean?"

At his raised eyebrow, she laughed. "Diapers. My mom kept an entire trunk full of my baby things for… later." She blushed and laughed again. "Mother was an eternal optimist."

Randi held out her arms, waiting for him to transfer the baby. It was a delicate maneuver, considering the precarious state of the towel he'd wrapped around his own waist and the blanket that kept slipping down his shoulders.

She laid the baby down on the rug in front of the fire and unwrapped the clumsily tied towel he'd used as a diaper. "Well, you didn't do so badly. With nothing else handy, the towel was actually a good idea."

"Necessity is the mother of invention," he murmured, chagrined at his own cliché but too beat to be clever.

Quickly and expertly Randi diapered Ricky and pulled a fuzzy yellow jumpsuit with a hood over his arms and legs. The kid would've looked like the Easter Bunny if he'd had floppy ears.

"His skin seems warm enough, but he's too quiet to suit me," she said.

"Yeah, I know what you mean. I've been thinking about that. I don't think he's in shock, his skin isn't clammy at all. But I'm concerned that he's dehydrated…or maybe even in the first stages of starvation. His belly looks distended to me."

She jerked around to face him and arched her brows in disbelief. "You think your own son might be starving?"

"He's not mine, Randi." It never occurred to him she might think Ricky was his child. After he'd blurted out the truth, he wondered if maybe he should have lied and spared himself a lot of trouble and explanations later.

"If he's not yours, what were you doing driving him around the countryside in the middle of a storm, and where's his mother?"

Yep. Good questions. Ones he wasn't positive he wanted to answer.

"Can we talk about that later? I'm a lawman, Randi, just trying to do a job. I promise, you're safe and I'll tell you everything eventually. But right now we need to find a way to get some liquids into the baby."

He had to hand it to her—Randi hesitated only a fraction of a second before she dug back into the basket. If he'd been in her shoes, he wasn't sure he'd have let the subject drop so fast. That fact alone made him wary, putting his instincts on alert.

She held up a glass baby bottle. "I found a few of these, but only one nipple that seems to be usable." Getting to her feet she said, "I have some distilled drinking water stashed away for emergencies. I suspect Ricky is well over six months and we can get by just washing the bottles instead of sterilizing them. It'll save a lot of time."

She handed him the baby and headed for the kitchen, turning back at the doorway for one last word. "But if you think we're done with the questions about this baby, better think again. I want answers."

In a few minutes she was back. Gently taking Ricky in her arms, she cradled him to her breast. It took a bit of coaxing to get him to take the bottle of water into his mouth, but soon the baby's instincts kicked in and he sucked mightily.

Manny breathed a sigh of relief at the tranquil sucking sounds. He'd made a promise to the baby to keep him safe and healthy, and by heaven, he intended to do everything in his power to see it through.

The sight of Randi holding the baby stirred something deep inside him that he had no business feeling. Long ago he'd buried his most basic needs—the need for the softness of a woman—the need for family. It had been several years since he'd contacted his own family, and he suddenly missed them more than he thought possible. He was sure that since he'd last seen them, his nieces and nephews would be nearly all grown up.

Manny positively refused to contemplate how long it had been since he'd felt the comfort of female companionship. But the sight of Randi and the baby seemed overwhelmingly erotic somehow. Man, when this mission was over, he'd better find himself some sweet little senorita. How long had it been, anyway?

"I've set a pan of water to boil on the stove," Randi whispered, trying not to disturb Ricky. "I think I've got a box of powdered milk on a shelf somewhere, too. If he can get this down, we can try a little milk."

Manny's gut wrenched as Randi concentrated on Ricky. There was an innocence about her that tugged at his conscience. Taking a breath, he systematically closed and locked off the physical and emotional needs that had been assaulting him. He needed to be strong and tough till he discovered her exact involvement in the baby-smuggling ring.

It didn't add up that she would be living alone. Someone that fragile-looking couldn't operate a working ranch by herself. So where was everybody?

He had no desire to hurt this ethereal young thing, but he had to do whatever necessary to find out if she was a suspect. It was part of the job.

* * *

Randi looked down at Ricky sleeping and felt a twinge of sadness in her heart. She was around children all the time at her nursery school job. Yet having a baby here, sleeping on her hearth and totally dependent on her for his well-being, seemed different. It reminded her too much of things she couldn't have—of things she'd probably have to bury forever.

Ricky took half the bottle of water and a full ounce of the powdered milk. When she'd placed him into the nest in the basket she'd made, he barely stirred.

His sweet face seemed so peaceful Randi began to relax. He'd lost that scrunched-up frightened look. She stroked his tiny hand, grateful that he no longer clutched it into a fist.

Meanwhile, Manny took her daddy's old clothes into the mud room to change. When he'd left the fireside, she'd felt a momentary chill, as if his leaving had changed the temperature and the physical forces swirling around her.

Shaking off the strange sensations, she tried to focus on the situation. She had a potentially sick child on her hands. The flooding river had no doubt cut them off from town for the time being. The phone wasn't working to call for help, and since they had no electricity to run the furnace's fan, they'd need to stay downstairs here near the fireplace or in the kitchen by the stove. And to top it all off, she still didn't know what Manny's relationship to this child might be.

Just who was this dangerous man, really, and why was he in her little town in the middle of a horrific rainstorm and flood? She'd be stuck throughout the emergency with a man who made her body alternate between shivers and hot sweats. What on earth had she gotten herself into?

If he wasn't Ricky's father, why was Manny in the car with the baby? What did his being a lawman have to do with Ricky? Randi had seen the way he treated the child, softly petting him and murmuring encouragement. She refused to think that he might have taken Ricky for a bad reason, but she was determined to get to the truth.

He was dangerous looking, what with the shaggy, ebony hair and the stubble darkening his chin and cheeks, but would it be fair to judge a man by appearances? She'd been taught never to jump to snap conclusions based on a person's looks.

"Is the baby asleep?"

Randi heard Manny's whispered words before she knew he was in the room and felt his hand on her shoulder. Instead of being startled, she felt heat settle over her in a liquid rush. Sort of like the burning sensation she'd experienced when she'd tried her one and only swallow of whisky but better...less bad tasting and more electric.

She nodded silently and lowered her chin to stare at the floor. Randi knew she couldn't look at him right now and still think clearly. Nervous tension made her body taut, and her mind fogged with unrealistic panic.

"You sure are handy to have around," he began in a soft and friendly tone.

Without looking up, she knew he'd eased himself down on the rug next to her. He wasn't touching her in any way, but she felt his presence tingling along the nerve endings of her skin. He was close enough that she could smell the cedar chips her mother had used to store her dad's clothes.

"I mean, you saved Ricky and me from drowning in the van and now you've taken us in and given us warmth and shelter from the storm. You've even come up with diapers and a baby bottle...and you know how to use them.'' He chuckled deep in his chest, the sexy rumbling vibrating inside her.

She peeked out from under her lashes to check his expression. When she saw his deep-set, chocolate-colored eyes flare to gold and his devastating features reflecting in the glow of the fire, she quivered with a strange anticipation. Randi felt a tide of color wash over her face, bathing her in a fiery flush and embarrassing her even more.

From the tips of his sock-clad feet to the top of his now-dry hair, the man reeked of power and sex.

Geez, she was way out of her depth here.

Manny watched the young woman sitting next to him while her skin turned from pale and cool to bright pink and heated. And his body reacted with a jolt of heat all its own. He understood about basic survival needs, about adrenaline causing lust and the need to reaffirm life, but that didn't explain the magnetic pull and his craving to protect her to his last breath.

He felt a bit more in control now that he'd changed and replaced his weapon in its hidden holster at his waist. He set his jaw and swallowed hard. She might be a suspect, and he must uncover her involvement in this international ring before they went any further. What did she know? It was urgent he find out.

He turned up the charm and tried a grin he certainly didn't feel. ''So, what were you really doing out on that lonely road tonight?''

''Hold on, there! I want my questions about you and the baby answered before we talk about anything else.''

''Look,'' he growled. ''I'm not asking out of idle curiosity, Randi. I'm a federal undercover agent, working on a case. And if I find out you're withholding information…or that you're involved in any way, I'll have you in custody so fast your head will swim."

Her terrified look should have told him all he needed to know. But his emotions were so raw he ignored his own gut instincts.

He pushed ahead, overpowering the conversation and demanding the truth with mere physical presence. "Now answer my question. Why were you out there alone tonight?" he persisted.

"I told you. I was coming home from work in Willow Springs. I'm a nursery school aide there." Her voice shook and the look in her eyes grew wilder as she automatically answered his demand.

"A pretty woman like you?" His hand went to her soft shoulder. "You sure you weren't there to meet someone?" He knew the grin had disappeared, but the longer she carried on this innocent game, the more Manny was positive she knew something she wasn't telling.

"N-n-n-no. Why are you asking? What kind of agent are you and what are you working on?" The words came pouring out. "It was just as I told you. Who would I be meeting in the middle of a storm?"

Manny groaned inwardly, wishing she didn't look so naive and young. He had to remain tough in the face of all this supposed innocence. She was either the best actress he'd ever seen or she was too guileless to be believed. His first quick impulse was that she must be one heck of an actress. He decided to force the truth out of her.

"All right. Let's go back to something else you said." He ended up having to clear his throat to continue. "You said no one lived here on the ranch with you. I find that hard to imagine."

"I...I didn't say that exactly."

Faster than a blink, Manny shoved the towel off her head. A rich, wet tangle of ash, gold and silver flowed over her shoulders. Grabbing a handful of it, he fisted his fingers into the silky strands. She gasped and her eyes opened to the size of dinner plates with his brash movement.

"Then what did you mean...exactly." He tugged her head back slowly, exposing the satiny skin on her slender neck to his view. A wayward thought of how much he'd like to place his lips on that expanse of softness flashed in his brain before he banished it and tried to steel his features into a threatening look.

"Let go of me! We...I...there's a ranch hand, uh, and his wife that live in the foreman's quarters. But..."

"So you lied to me?" he demanded.

"No! You didn't ask about the ranch. You asked about the house. Now let go...please."

Manny saw the tears welling in her eyes and immediately released his grip on her hair. But his hand refused to let the damp tresses go completely. His fingers lingered in the intoxicating texture of the multicolored silk.

He felt like a jerk for hurting her. But it *was* part of the job, and he had to finish his interrogation. Ricky's life might depend on finding the answers.

"Why all these questions?" she sobbed. "What's going on? I haven't done anything wrong." Randi sniffed and touched a finger to the corner of her eye.

"I don't want to hurt you." His voice sounded raspy, hoarse. "But I'm the one asking the questions here. And I mean to know the truth. All of it."

She arched her eyebrows and glanced away as if she was barely interested in this whole conversation. Damn her. He wanted her scared—scared and willing to tell him anything she might know. He was finished playing games.

Manny had his Glock out of its holster before he had a chance to think it through. "Who else lives on this ranch? Tell me," he demanded. "And you'd better make sure I believe you."

Her eyes widened and her hands jumped to cover that full mouth, probably to keep a scream from escaping her lips. Now he'd done it. He reholstered his weapon instantly. Drawing a weapon was just an ingrained movement whenever he needed an intimidating tactic.

This time he hadn't really been prepared to shoot, however. The monumental significance of that potentially deadly oversight wasn't lost on him. Nothing like that had ever happened to him before.

"Please. I'll tell you anything you want to know. Only…please keep that gun out of sight."

Randi forced a sob back down her throat. She refused to let him see her panic. Dear Lord, was she going to go to jail because she'd been a Good Samaritan? Lewis Lee always said that no good deed goes unpunished. She prayed she'd be around long enough to tell him he was right.

Manny softened his expression. Funny, but she could swear that this big macho man looked remorseful—guilty even. The gun had disappeared under his shirt at his waist almost as quickly as it had appeared. Randi's gut told her that he would never have used it on her. Her fears subsided the instant she'd seen his expression. Meanwhile, he silently waited for her to continue.

How odd that all her fears had melted away. He was still a huge, dangerous man sitting in her front room and wearing a gun that he didn't seem to mind using. But there was a glint of some emotion in his eyes that comforted her, drew her to him. Made her positive he was really the lawman he professed to be.

"My…" Her voice cracked and she started over. "My stepfather lives on another part of the ranch. On the Cottonwood section. But he won't be helping us if that's what you're thinking. Probably wouldn't help—even if he could reach us. He's kind of put out with me these days." She swallowed and tried to soothe her dry throat. It was no use. "Besides, he hasn't been around in a couple of months. Not since…my mother's funeral."

"Your mother just died?"

She nodded. The emotion in his eyes changed to sympathy, and her head swam with confusion. What kind of man was this? And what did he really want from her?

# Three

A multitude of emotions raced through Randi when Manny stood, turned and stretched out a hand to help her stand. She'd seen the guilt in his eyes when he'd fisted his hands in her hair, questioning her.

His look clearly told her he believed his actions had caused her pain. What she'd actually felt was simply fear—not physical discomfort. He hadn't hurt her, just scared her. That Manny had such a sympathetic and honest streak in him was as clear as if it was painted on his forehead.

And now…

Now that he wanted to take her hand, wanted to touch her again, she hesitated. She'd been so concerned about the baby's welfare that she'd given in to Manny's demands too easily. For some reason she'd let him take total control.

All right, so he said he was a lawman and she'd believed him immediately. That might have been part of it. Believing what he said might be stupid of her, but she knew she would eventually get the answers. There was just something about him that made her know he could be trusted in the long run.

But for right now she marveled at how quickly her fear had disappeared. Past the fear, past the consuming questions in her heart about who he really was and what he wanted, Randi had felt alive and sensual. For the first time in her life, she actually wanted a man's touch. Wanted it bad.

Not just any man, mind you. Randi wanted this man. He was all she'd ever dreamed about—dangerous but sexy. In Randi's eyes he was a perfect combination of Zorro and some exotic and romantic pirate.

The problem was, she had no idea how to go about getting him. For ten years she'd buried her needs, smothered her desires. First there'd been her mother's stroke, then her stepfather's physical abandonment. Finally came the unrelenting pressure of seeing to her mother's needs while trying to keep the ranch afloat. All of that left precious little time for Randi to have any kind of life.

If it hadn't been for Lewis Lee and his wife, Hannah, Randi wouldn't have graduated from high school. And if it hadn't been for Marian Baker, the librarian, bringing her books every week after graduation, Randi would have withered and blown away. Reading had been her lifeline, her connection to the outside world.

Marian had even arranged for Randi to take care of a couple of toddlers while their mothers worked. The small job meant she could be in the house when her disabled mother needed her. It also meant that temporarily there had been enough cash to keep from having to sell off the land. Despite the puny allowance and doctor's bills her stepfather had paid, there was never enough money to go around.

"I'm afraid you and I are stuck with each other for the duration of the storm, Randi. I'd appreciate it if we could stick close to each other for the baby's safety as well as our own." Manny eyed her with a piercing look when she still hesitated to move. "Come on into the kitchen with us. I think we need something in our stomachs.

"I won't hurt you ever again. I promise." He tucked his hand into the pocket of his jeans and bunched up his face with a look of pure helplessness when she still made no move.

"I know I didn't act very civilized before," he began again. "But I did apologize. Can't we make a new start? Maybe we could talk...get to know each other better. Please?"

Oh, yeah. Randi wanted desperately to know him better. Her gaze traveled down the length of him, taking in her daddy's chambray work shirt stretched tightly across Manny's broad chest. He'd left the top three buttons open. She doubted they'd cover his muscles, anyway, but open like that they left nearly half of his torso in plain view. She stared at the dark, curly hair covering his bronzed skin and gulped.

Her fingers shook reflexively at the sight of his chest, and she fisted them to keep still. She'd never in her life seen anything quite so compelling. With a supreme effort at controlling her urges, she forced herself not to jump up and test the feel of his body. Her good sense told her to be careful—to go slow.

Talk about uncivilized. What she wanted right now definitely qualified as primal.

When she could pull away from the sight of all that skin, she dropped her gaze down the rest of him—across the leather belt he'd used to draw her father's jeans tight and on down past the bulging mound of him encased in soft, well-washed blue denim.

*Oh, my.*

That view finally put her in motion. She turned, while carefully managing to avoid touching Manny.

"Do you like coffee? I can make some. It's time I added wood to the stove, anyway." She figured she was babbling, but couldn't seem to stop.

"Yeah. I could go for coffee," he murmured, picking up the baby's basket and following her into the kitchen.

Manny wondered how he could ever make up for behaving like such an idiot. What had gotten into him? The young woman who'd just put coffee on the stove to boil was obviously innocent.

In eight years of undercover work he'd developed a life-saving instinct for detecting lies. He was usually right on target. His gut screamed at him for ever doubting her. Perhaps someone else on the ranch was involved with baby smugglers, but she wasn't. Of that he was now positive. He doubted she'd ever even heard about such things.

While Randi scrambled some eggs using the same stove that heated the room and warmed their coffee, Manny fought to bring peace into the tension that surrounded the two stranded strangers and baby. "Can I do anything to help?"

She looked at him with amazement shining in her eyes.

"What? You don't think I can cook?" he asked with a chuckle. "I'll have you know my *abuela* insisted that all members of her family, male and female alike, should know how to take care of themselves.''

He found the bread bin and removed two slices of whole wheat. ''It's a real handy talent, and sometimes even fun.''

Manny glanced around the room looking for cooking utensils and supplies. Finally he gave Randi a questioning look. Where did she keep things, anyway?

Obviously mistaking his intentions, Randi shook her head at him. ''Do you think you can toast that bread without the electric toaster?'' Her lips curled at the corners in an adorable smirk.

''Can I have one egg and a little of Ricky's milk?''

''Yes, but…''

''Then stand aside, woman, and watch a master at work.''

Manny busied himself, frying the bread over her open-flamed stovetop while Randi set the table. As he worked, he went over in his head the events that had brought him to this point.

What the hell had happened to this mission, anyway? His Operation Rock-a-Bye assignment had been to go undercover in Mexico until he ingratiated himself with a group of undocumented immigrants making their way to the border. He'd picked a group with several small children, and although they'd never fully trusted him, he'd been able to keep track of them through their travels. Even when they'd hooked up with a particularly nasty band of *coyotes*, dangerous men hired to bring them across the river, the little group of Mexican nationals continued to allow his shadow to fall on their campsites.

Manny had hoped that once they'd crossed the border he could manage to get them to confide in him, give him the critical information he needed to infiltrate the smugglers gang. He'd heard that this particular group of immigrants knew of children taken from their homeland and spirited to the U.S. Around a campfire one night, he'd even overheard a disagreement about one family receiving money in exchange for a baby.

When the illegals he'd befriended crossed the Rio Grande and broke into smaller bands, he followed one family who moved alone into the interior of Texas with their *coyote*. What Manny hadn't known, or even guessed, was that the *coyotes* they'd hired were also members of the baby smuggling ring.

He'd discovered the truth too late.

And that was when this whole assignment had fallen apart. He didn't know what to do to put it right again. He only knew that some things would forever be wrong, and that the last thing he needed was an innocent civilian like Randi in the middle of the investigation.

He flipped the bread out of the pan and onto the plates she'd already loaded with scrambled eggs. "There you go."

She sat down at the worn-out looking wooden table next to the stove and took a bite. "Mmm. It's good."

Manny thought she looked good enough to eat herself. In the past hour, he'd quit thinking of her as a frail little waif and started appreciating her firm, lithe body and the sexual energy coming from every pore.

"Don't sound so surprised. If you'd had some cornmeal, I would've really made you a treat."

Randi smiled at him before she took another bite of food. Manny watched as her full, pouty lips covered the fork. She slowly pulled the empty tines back again, moaning in satisfaction as she swallowed.

With her sensual sound of pleasure, his libido went

on full alert. Suddenly he could think of nothing but tracing those silken lips with his own, dipping his tongue into that ripe mouth and tasting her, and having her taste him in return.

He could feel the sinew in his muscles tense up. When he saw her flick that rose-tipped tongue over slightly parted lips to clean off any crumbs, it was all he could do not to use his own tongue to follow hers. He had to swallow hard to keep the groan, rumbling deep in his chest, from escaping his throat.

Watching her, being this close to all that femininity was pure torment. Desire had never hit him in the middle of an assignment. Why now?

He spun around to see about Ricky, who still slept in the basket on the kitchen counter. He tried hard to remember that all of this was just another mission.

"Aren't you going to eat? It's delicious," she asked.

"Uh, yeah," he managed through a clenched jaw. "I just wanted to check the baby. He's awfully quiet."

"I plan on changing him and seeing if he'll take a little more milk as soon as we're done. I want to let him sleep as long as possible. Please come sit down and eat. I thought you said you wanted to talk."

*Talk?* All of a sudden the whole concept seemed beyond his comprehension.

Manny squeezed his eyes shut and drew a steadying breath before he turned around to face her. "Right. While I eat, why don't you tell me why a pretty young girl is living out here all by herself? Why hasn't some nice cowpoke swept you off your feet by now?"

Randi must have recognized a sidestepping dodge when she heard one. "Wait a minute. I've already been through one interrogation. I'm not saying any more until you tell me about yourself. Who is Ricky to you? And what were you two doing on the low-water bridge road in the middle of a storm?''

Manny's mind tried to come up with a plausible lie, but he was too wiped out to concentrate. Besides, from some deeply buried spot inside him, a strong voice demanded that he not lie to this woman. But why she caused such a powerful internal command stumped him.

As long as he'd been in this job, his conscience had never once stopped him from fabricating a story. Why did he hesitate now? When he'd been a much younger man, he'd even spun a few stories *not* in the line of work—for the pretty ladies.

Of course, he hadn't told white lies like that for quite a number of years. Hadn't needed to really. Lately, the women with whom he'd had relationships didn't need to be persuaded. They'd been just as happy as he had to spend a few hours together away from the storms of life and then move on, with no regrets and no looking back.

So what was so different about Randi? Even in his exhausted state, Manny knew what the problem was. The look in her eyes said she wanted forever. Oh, she probably would deny it, and might not even know it about herself, but Randi was not the kind to have a fling or a casual relationship. The truth of that was written all over her.

In his business "forever" could be no more than a heartbeat away.

Manny beat back his budding desires, and decided to fudge with half the truth. "I can't tell you everything you want to know, Randi."

When she rolled her eyes and set her chin, he knew he'd have to give up a morsel of the story—something to settle her fears at least. "Really. Just believe that I *am* a lawman, and I've been undercover on assignment.

Even telling you that much might jeopardize years' worth of work, but for your own safety, you must trust me.''

In the flickering glow of the lamplight he saw her eyes had turned pale green. They widened with shock before they quickly narrowed in disbelief. ''Trust you? I don't even know you. First you interrogate me like I'm some kind of criminal, then you put a gun in my face, and now you tell me to believe you're undercover? You expect me to just quietly let everything slide and accept it?'' Randi stood, swept up both their plates and strode to the sink, effectively rejecting him as she turned her back.

Without facing him, she demanded at least one straight answer. ''What about Ricky? Why was he in the van with you, and where are his parents?''

Manny sighed and absently rubbed at the ache in his shoulder. She must accept knowing only part of the story. All of it would be too much for her right now. The whole truth might also be very dangerous.

''I wasn't in the van, Randi. I was chasing it. Ricky had been…taken…by the man driving.''

''Taken? Like in kidnapped, you mean?'' She spun to face him, clasping her hands in front of her chest.

He nodded and watched her expression, fascinated by such open emotion. Manny could see her making connections and piecing together the frayed ends of what he'd told her. She was too damn bright, he finally decided.

Being too smart could get her killed. He'd rather keep the nastiness of this whole situation from touching her.

''If you were chasing the van, where was your car? I didn't see another vehicle on the road.'' She only hesitated a fraction of a second. "And what happened to the van's driver?"

"My bike slid off the side of the road when I stopped to help. I'm not positive about what happened to the driver...except I think he must have been thrown out when the van went over. I doubt he escaped alive, but as soon as the storm subsides we'll find out."

Randi made a strangled, hiccupy sound and moved to Ricky's basket. "Oh, my God." She bent to pick up the baby and held him closely to her chest.

"Don't ask me any more," he mumbled. "Tomorrow, when the storm clears, we'll notify the sheriff about the accident and the driver. I'll find my Hog, and Ricky and I will be on our way out of your life."

Randi closed her eyes and leaned her cheek against Ricky's hair.

Manny watched closely while Randi changed Ricky. She coaxed the boy into taking a little more milk while Manny rinsed the dishes in cold water and stacked them in the sink. Her ancient, hot-water heater wouldn't start without electricity. He wondered why she didn't have an emergency generator like most ranches did these days.

To conserve dry wood for what might be a long, cold night, they moved back into the front room, settling Ricky's basket near the fire. It was the only place in the house that would be warm enough to keep the baby safe.

While Manny stoked the fire, Randi started to place the basket by the hearth, appeared to change her mind and carried it a few feet back, then stood hesitating in the middle of the room.

"Stop fussing, set the basket down anywhere and settle in. We've got a long night ahead of us," he said. Finally she seemed to find a spot that suited her. Manny couldn't help but smile at how much like a mother hen she was.

When she bent down to tuck in the baby, Manny studied the room in the gleaming light of the roaring fire. The jagged rock fireplace soared into the raised beamed ceiling. The effect was really quite stunning.

The fireplace rocks and heavy wood beams were obviously old and set by hand. Each stone had been fitted to match the others and then mortared tightly in place, while the solid wood beams had been pegged together in the manner of the early settlers. He wondered how long this house had stood here on the range.

The furnishings in this front room were also old, and some of the oak pieces bore hand-hewn marks. Each table must have been lovingly polished to a shiny gloss by someone who cared about fine wood as much as he always had.

The one stuffed sofa in the room had been covered with a quilt, another handmade piece, if Manny was any judge. And everywhere that was visible in the light bouncing around the room, there were tender little touches. Framed pictures of smiling people on the table by the sofa. Tiny dried-flower-filled vases on the shelf and tray table in the corner. Square, hand-embroidered pillows artfully placed here and there.

Randi finished hovering over Ricky and plopped down on the rug in front of the hearth next to Manny. Quietly she stared into the fire, hugging her knees to her chest.

The glow of incandescent firelight radiated, making her skin shimmer. And making Manny wish he could be someone else for one night. At first he wished he was the kind of man who deserved to know a woman like Randi. To be the kind of steady homebody who would stick around for a lifetime just to watch the light in her eyes.

But as the heat from the fire danced across his skin, he began wishing he was another kind of man. The kind that could take what he was sure she'd readily give and then leave without a backward glance. A man who didn't mind giving and receiving pleasure from an unsophisticated and naive girl. A man without conscience. A man like he'd always imagined himself to be.

"You look exhausted," he heard himself whisper. "Why don't you lie down on the couch? I'll be fine here with a blanket or two. I can keep an eye on Ricky and the fire, maybe catch a few winks before daybreak."

Shaking her head, Randi ignored Manny's words and found herself hypnotized by the blue and orange lights of the vacillating flames. This night had been the most fantastic adventure of her whole life, and she didn't want it to end until she had a chance to get closer to the fascinating man she'd taken in.

She'd been able to help save a child. Her dull little world had been blown apart by adrenaline rushes and danger, and to add to all that, she was now about to spend the entire night with an intriguing and sexy man she would never see again after tomorrow.

She tried to steady her nerves by taking deep breaths, but that only increased the tension swirling through her veins. Inexperienced though she was, Randi was positive a man like this would come on to her. At least she hoped he might. But right away...? Or would he drive her crazy waiting?

Why couldn't she be the type of woman who knew how to make a man do what she wanted? She'd never lingered on the regrets of her life. Had never coveted anything except a college education. Never…until Manny and Ricky had dropped into the picture.

"Randi? Please rest. I don't want to have to worry about you taking sick after we leave."

She could barely believe he'd care one way or the other about her welfare after he'd gone. The idea of him even giving a single thought to her when he left warmed her soul. Hungry for kindness and caring, Randi felt her nervousness melt, replaced by tingling anticipation. This man wouldn't hurt her. The look she'd seen in his eyes the last time he imagined he'd caused her pain made her sure of it.

"I'll take the couch," she mumbled, moving to it and reclining into her grandmother's favorite quilt. "But can we talk for a while? I'm still all keyed up from the flood."

"Sure. I'd like to learn a little bit about the background of this house and what you're doing here with no family."

"It's not a very interesting story, but if you want something to bore you to sleep, I guess I can oblige."

Manny chuckled softly and leaned back on his elbows. "Who built this house, and how long has it been here?" he inquired lazily.

"My great-great-grandfather first homesteaded the place. He came to Texas with his parents right after the Civil War. A few years later he settled here on the Edwards Plateau with his wife and new baby. They built the house together, carved it out of the rock and trees that covered the land."

Randi drew the quilt over her body and snuggled down into the sofa cushions. She poured out the ranch's history.

Looking around the shadowed room, she could see

past the walls to the deterioration destroying her family home. Her heart ached for the spirits of her ancestors, looking down from above and seeing the disintegration of their homestead within sight.

"What about you?" he asked. "You said your mother just passed away and that you had a stepfather nearby? Tell me the story of Randi Cullen."

"Hah. Another dull tale, I'm afraid." She closed her eyes and lowered her voice. "My daddy died when I was ten. He was the best thing in my life and when he was gone, most of the fun went with him. My mother was good to me, but she had to work very hard to keep the ranch going alone.

"I watched the lines grow on her face as she struggled to keep our heads above water. I hurt for her, but I didn't know how to help. All I knew was that we had promised my father that this land would always stay in the family."

The fire snapped and flared as a log broke, cutting into her thoughts and reminding her suddenly that very likely she was the last of her family. There wouldn't be another generation of Cullens on the land. In fact, the way things were going, as the last Cullen she might not even be able to save it in this generation.

"Anyway…" She cleared her throat. "When I was thirteen, my mother married a man by the name of Frank Riley from Willow Springs. I don't think she loved him, but he was an attorney. He'd drawn up my daddy's will and he was the executor for the estate. I'm sure she thought he'd help with the ranch…that he'd save us and the land. But I guess he never really cared much about any of it."

Randi yawned and opened her eyes to see if Manny

was listening. He was still propped up on an elbow, but she couldn't tell if he was paying attention.

"Less than a year later, Mother had her first stroke and was paralyzed on the entire left side of her body. She never left her wheelchair after that. Frank said he couldn't bear watching his formerly vibrant wife dying, so he built himself a house on a different section of the ranch property and moved out. He'd traveled to Mexico and other places on business a lot, anyway. So I didn't miss him at all.

"I believe it was a relief for him to shed himself of the Cullen influence in this house. I felt sorry for him trying to live up to Daddy and the whole family's reputation."

Well, that wasn't strictly true. She'd felt sorry for Frank right up until her mother died: he'd inherited half the ranch and had immediately started demanding she agree to sell out to a developer. The truth was, she probably couldn't hold out much longer against his badgering and her inexperience at running a ranch.

Randi heard her words begin to drift away and gave in to the drowsiness overtaking her. Right before the comfort of sleep temporarily turned her world dark, she could have sworn she heard Manny murmuring softly.

"Sleep well, sweet Randi. You've been strong and brave long enough. Let someone else fight the dark angels for one night. I'm here to protect you."

It seemed like only a few minutes later when something awoke her. The fire was nearly out. Randi sat up, intending to stir the embers and add a log. A long, low moan suddenly pierced the silence of the room, frightening her and adding to the chill. What on earth?

In the dim shadows of the room she saw Manny jump to his feet. "What was that noise?" he demanded.

''I'm not sure. Do you think it might be the storm?''
She rolled off the couch. ''Sounds like the wind,
but—''

Her words were cut short as the moan turned into a
loud, thundering crackle. From somewhere above her,
Randi heard a ripping and tearing sound. Dear Lord,
what more could happen tonight?

# Four

____

Randi grabbed a flashlight from the drawer and flicked it on before handing it to Manny. She paused only long enough to check on the baby, then turned to follow Manny up the stairs in search of the source of trouble.

She came up behind him as they met at the top of the three flights.

"Do you have any idea what made that noise?" he asked.

She was almost out of breath from fear and the mad dash up the stairs but managed a shaky reply. "I'm afraid I do."

After they'd reached the attic doorway, Manny twisted the flashlight, throwing a beam of light around the room and finding what Randi had feared. A good chunk of the roof's west corner had been torn away, exposing a portion of the attic to the elements. The rain blew down through the hole in pulverizing waves.

It was as bad as could be. The destruction of her family home had begun in earnest—board by board. Randi sank to her knees.

"I can't do it anymore," she whimpered. "I just can't. I give up." She had nothing left to fight with. What her stepfather hadn't been able to accomplish by demanding she sell, the elements had.

It was over.

Randi felt Manny's hands on her shoulders. The rain had soaked her, and she trembled as he dragged her off the floor.

"What can we do? Can we temporarily plug the hole?" He had to shout to be heard over the wind and rain.

She shook her head, desperately sick of trying.

"Randi!" Manny gave her shoulders a little shake. "Randi, answer me. Is there a tarp, or some plywood we can make do as a patch till the storm blows over? How about tools? Where are your tools?"

She could barely understand the words he used. Randi felt as if she'd been dropped into the depths of an ocean. Her vision blurred, and his garbled voice wove in and out.

Manny took her breath away by suddenly dragging her to him, tightly crushing her to his chest. He used one hand to cup the back of her head and moved his cheek alongside hers.

The comfort and warmth overwhelmed her. It had been so long since anyone had held her. Not since her father died.

"Oh, sugar, don't fall apart on me now," he breathed into her ear. "We can handle this, Randi. I can fix it, but I need your help."

"There's nothing…" Even though she'd shouted, she knew her voice was drowned out by the storm.

He was too close—too close for her to think clearly, so she used her palms to push away from his chest, but he didn't release her from his embrace. Pulling her head back to see his expression, Randi was shocked to see the intensity illuminating his eyes.

For one crazy moment she thought he was going to kiss her. In contrast to the violence swirling around them, he reached out with his forefinger to tenderly touch her face. He lightly drew a line down her cheek.

Riveted to his gaze and with his strength pouring into her through his touch, Randi dragged herself out of her depression. "There's a toolshed alongside the house." He'd given her the one miracle she'd needed the most—hope.

"Maybe we'll find something we can use." She strained against his hold until he finally released her. "Come on." Feeling strangely bereft at the loss of his warmth, she shook off the sensation long enough to act. "I'll show you."

Randi directed Manny to the toolshed before she dashed back into the front room to check on Ricky and to stoke the fire. The baby seemed cool to her touch and murmured in his sleep as she tucked the blanket around him. She hoped those were all good signs.

Once she satisfied herself as to Ricky's condition and safety, Randi quickly donned her slicker and rushed out to help Manny in the shed. By the time she reached him, he'd located the tools he needed and was thrashing around trying to find something with which to patch the roof.

"Here. Hold the light for me, will you?" he shouted over the pounding sounds of rain against the toolshed.

She took the heavy flashlight from him and aimed the beam around the crowded shed. ''I don't see anything we can use,'' she volunteered.

Randi saw nothing but rusty, old tools and equipment—except, of course, years' worth of accumulated dust and cobwebs. ''There may be some used plywood in the barn, but...''

''We don't have time to find it,'' Manny warned. ''If we don't plug the hole right now, the water will soak through the floorboards and ruin the room below.''

Despair and defeat nearly did her in once again. But right before she totally gave up, she was astonished to see Manny tugging on the heavy door to the shed with his good arm.

''Shine that light over here on the hinges,'' he demanded.

She did as he asked, but was confused at his intent. ''What are you...?''

''Can you hand me the hammer? I think we can break these old hinges loose, but we'll have to work together.''

''Okay, but...'' As she picked up the hammer and turned it over to him, his idea became suddenly clear. ''You think we can use the door to plug the roof?''

''You'd rather have wet old tools than a flood inside your house, wouldn't you?'' He hit the top hinge with a couple of jarring blows, and the rusty metal fell away. Another couple of raps disintegrated the bottom hinge.

''Now we've got a small problem,'' he hollered. ''I can't hold the door and get rid of the last hinge by myself. My injured shoulder will give out. If I start it for you, do you think you can break off the middle hinge while I lean on the door?''

At this point Randi might have given her life trying to help him. He was so intense and so positive that what he was doing would work. She nodded, never thinking that he might not be able to see the small move in the darkness.

He saw enough. Immediately he gave the remaining metal a gentle tap to weaken it.

"Hold the flashlight with one hand so you can see where you're aiming, then hit it as hard as you can with the other," he ordered, giving her the hammer.

While Manny braced himself against the old wood of the door, Randi took a deep breath and tried to concentrate on the spot she needed to hit.

"Ready?" he asked.

"As I'll ever be," she responded, taking a swing.

The first blow only glanced off the hinge, and she groaned in frustration.

"Try it again, sweetheart. You can do it. Focus."

Her second attempt broke through the rusted metal. The hinge gave way while the bulky door eased down against Manny's body. He used his good shoulder to steady one side of the door and managed to use the other hand to grab lower on the other side.

"I can handle it, if you'll bring the tools and open the doors ahead of me," he said.

Randi gathered the tools as fast as she could and led the way back up the stairs to the attic. It boggled her mind to think of him hefting the heavy wood, but when she glanced back to check on him, he didn't look as if he was having any trouble. She could see his arm muscles flexing easily underneath her daddy's old work shirt. The sight enthralled her.

Lifting the door into place turned out to be a much more difficult task than getting it upstairs.

"We'll need heavy rope. Can you locate some while

I move these boxes around to stand on?'' he asked while he leaned the old door against the wall.

"Sure. I saw some rope up here the other day. I'll find it.''

With Randi's help, Manny rigged up a pulley system and leveraged the shed's door to the roof. She was fascinated to find how easily he worked with the partial use of one arm and with the rain beating down on him the whole time. The man truly was a dynamo.

Randi had to turn away from Manny a couple of times to keep from fantasizing about him right in the middle of a crisis. Good heavens, she could certainly become very foolish if she didn't watch her step.

After he'd wrangled the door into place, Manny hammered a couple of nails into each side to temporarily keep it steady. Randi stuffed a heavy old quilt into the broken corner. Finally they were standing, once again, under a shelter from the storm. The last thing she did was run downstairs to retrieve the mop and bucket from the pantry.

"Let me do that for you,'' he muttered, as she began to swing the heavy mop around the floor.

"It's not necessary. I can do it. Besides you've done so much already. You must be exhausted.''

"This was nothing compared to what I can do with two good shoulders, sugar.'' He gently took the handle from her hands. "There's a half foot of water on the floor in spots. I'll work with the mop. You go get as many towels and rags as you can find. We'll dry it up in no time.''

At last, when the floor was barely damp, Randi looked up from her kneeling position to find Manny resting on the mop handle, studying her.

"We make a good team. You know that, Randi Cullen?"

She stood to face him, pondering the meaning of his words. Darn, she sure wished she'd had more experience with men. Was he trying to tell her something? He'd sounded as if he wanted to be her friend, but did he really mean it that way?

Manny leaned the mop handle against a wall and stepped closer to her. Randi's heart began to beat faster, rushing blood to parts of her body that she hadn't before realized existed. She nearly squirmed away, but instead held herself still. She refused to be a coward.

He placed both hands on her shoulders and moved closer still. "Have you forgiven me for hurting you earlier?"

His breath warmed her forehead, making her ache for things impossible to name. She couldn't speak so she tried to move into the shelter of his open arms.

Her legs refused to work, making her immobile and totally frustrated. Being in his arms was all she'd been able to think about since the first moment he'd climbed into her truck. So why was she so hesitant now?

To her everlasting relief, Manny inched closer, draping his muscular arms around her and letting them capture her in his embrace. "Yes, I can see in your eyes that you have."

His voice sounded like a warm smile, but his eyes were deadly serious as he leaned his forehead down to rest against hers. She inhaled a steadying breath and found herself responding to the scent of work and sweat from him that wound its way down her torso and landed in her belly.

She was embarrassed to be so needy and full of desire for him. Where had her self-respect gone?

She realized all of a sudden that self-respect simply didn't matter. Good riddance, she thought with a half smile.

For her whole life she'd dreamed about being this close to a man who could shake up her dull world. And here he was.

Helplessly Randi placed her hands on his chest. She'd wanted to touch him, but where did one put one's hands at a time like this?

With her first touch, Manny sighed. "I have no real excuse for my actions. I should have known you were as innocent as you seemed."

Randi's hands fisted tightly in his shirt. She sensed a change in him and raised her chin, slanting her head to better see his expression. The move put her mouth only inches away from his.

"And I have absolutely no excuse for this, either," he whispered.

Before Randi could prepare, Manny lowered his mouth, placed his lips squarely against hers and kissed her. Instinctively she responded by opening her lips to give him better access—and got the ride of a lifetime.

Little tingles shot to every inch of her body as if she'd been dropped into a bottle of soda pop. After the first warmth-filled moment, Manny seemed to hesitate by pulling back slightly. When Randi moaned with regret at the loss of his pressing attentions, he dragged her tighter to him and covered her lips once more. An inkling of the meaning of womanly power flashed through her.

She lifted her arms to thread her fingers through his hair. The sensuous feeling of silk nearly buckled her knees.

This time Manny's lips grazed across hers with soft

brush strokes. Over and over. Heat upon heat. His gentle assault took her by surprise. She could barely believe such tenderness came from someone so strong. His tongue softly traced her lips.

Liquid warmth filled her with hazy longings. Without thinking, she opened her mouth for him and luxuriated in the brand-new sensations caused when the tip of his tongue tentatively explored hers.

Suddenly the hazy longings turned into crystal-clear needs. Her breasts, pressed tightly against his chest, began to ache and swell. She jammed herself tighter against him and couldn't help but compare the hardness of his body to the growing softness of her own.

Randi tried to focus on all the feelings surrounding and coursing through her. She wanted desperately to capture every emotion, every nuance. This might be her only shot at being turned on by a man, and she needed to remember each detail. Her last coherent thought before she lost herself to the moment was to wonder what the repercussions of making love with a desperado might be.

Manny was past all clear reasoning. Vaguely, somewhere in the back of his brain, he knew what he was doing was stupid—careless. But he just couldn't stop. Not yet.

She responded to him like no other woman ever had before, trusting him not to hurt her and opening herself to whatever he wanted to do. His hands itched to touch her, to feel the shimmering smoothness of her skin as he ran his fingers over all her hidden spots.

Dumb bastard, he berated himself. This nice young girl needed protection, not a thoughtless seduction. He suddenly felt ashamed and ended the kiss.

Manny couldn't bring himself to take a step back from her, however. He continued to hold her steady, watching while she opened her eyes, blinked a few times and tried to focus on his face.

The sight of her moist lips, slightly parted, drew his hand magically to her face. He traced her bottom lip with his thumb.

"Uh, maybe we'd better stop right here," he mumbled.

Randi closed her eyes and shrugged her shoulders. That slight gesture nearly undid his resolve. He leaned in for one last kiss.

A baby's wail broke through the stillness and Manny halted in midair. *Dios mio.* In his lust he'd forgotten all about Operation Rock-a-Bye, the deadly storm and... Ricky.

After dashing down the stairs with Randi, Manny pulled up short at the threshold to the front room. What he saw was unnerving and left him shaking his head. There, still in his basket, but sitting up and roaring at the top of his lungs, was a much improved Ricky.

Randi was at the baby's side in an instant. Hauling him up into her arms, she shushed him while patting his bottom.

"Hush now, lamby. Everything's going to be just fine," she murmured.

No longer the scared little rabbit with promises in her eyes, Randi's whole being had changed. Manny openly stared at a woman totally in her element. Mothering apparently came naturally.

He touched his fingers to his lips, remembering the way hers had felt against them. He needed to get ahold of himself. Actually, he badly needed to get away from her and the temptation she represented.

Manny followed the two of them into the kitchen. When he entered the cozy warmth of the flower-wallpapered room, he realized the rain had quieted and that murky daylight had begun seeping past the steely gray clouds.

Morning. The worst of the storm must be over. He and Ricky could leave. Just go. Get away.

That's what he wanted. Right?

He stood beside them as Randi broke off a piece of banana and handed it to Ricky, who immediately stuffed the whole thing in his mouth and grinned.

"Uh-oh." She stuck her fingers in the baby's mouth and pulled out part of the gooey mess. "Too much at one time. Chew it up first."

"Chew?" Manny asked, trying to ignore the war going on inside him.

"Sure." Randi pried open Ricky's mouth and proudly pointed at a couple of tiny pearly colored baby teeth.

"Well, I'll be damned."

She chuckled at his surprise. "He's a big boy."

Ricky grinned, flapping his arms and using all his charming talent to beg for another bite of banana. Randi obliged him with a smaller piece this time.

"He's a doll, isn't he?" she cooed. "I'll bet his parents are frantic. Will you be taking him back to them as soon as you can leave here?"

Manny's stony silence jolted her. She felt her smile fade as she grabbed Ricky up in her arms and tried to remain calm.

"You will notify them as soon as the phone's working...won't you?" She'd tried to keep the shakes out of her voice, but noticed a quaver in her words just the same.

"I can't, Randi." Manny's voice sounded a little

rough around the edges, too. "They…they're dead. Murdered by…"

A rap on the back door startled them both, and they jerked toward the sound.

Randi's knees were weak and her stomach turned somersaults. Dead? Murdered?

Manny grabbed the baby up in his arms. "Who's that?"

She fought to find some composure. "How would I know? Maybe it's Lewis Lee come to check up on me."

As she started toward the mud room door, Manny gripped her shoulder with one hand. "Where can we hide? No one should see us here."

The baby started to fuss and she knew that hiding them in time would be impossible. She shook her head. "It's too late for that."

Blindly she twisted her shoulder away, heading through the mud room toward the door and whoever might be on the other side.

"Wait." Manny was at her side in an instant. "Please don't give me away, sugar. I have a job to do. Can you tell whoever it is that we're long-lost relatives or something?"

He leaned down, keeping the baby between them, and lasered a quick, searing kiss across her lips. "I'll see that the ones responsible for killing Ricky's parents pay, Randi. But I need time, and we don't know who we can trust. Help me to help Ricky."

She turned toward the door once more, stunned by the kiss as much as by his words. The knocking grew more insistent.

"Please?" Staying close behind her, he lightly touched her elbow as she reached for the doorknob.

She straightened her back and opened the door, half-afraid of what she'd find on the other side.

"Morning, Randi. How'd you weather the storm?" Deputy Wade Reese stood, hat in hand, with a slight smile and the typically too-earnest expression he normally wore on his face.

"Deputy Reese." Her usual feelings of warmth for the easy-going deputy sheriff were tempered by the fact that Manny and the baby stood only a few feet behind her.

"I know you've been cut off since last night. Thought I'd better stop by to check now that the storm's let up. May I come in? Promise I won't get mud on anything."

The genial, slightly overweight deputy stepped inside before Randi could gather her wits and think of an excuse to keep him out. Why was it that everyone she knew figured they could just traipse into her house without a moment's notice? Living in one place all her life had developed into a real trial, she fumed.

She slammed the door shut and spun, but it was too late.

"Well, hey there," the deputy drawled as he came face-to-face with Manny and Ricky.

Manny said nothing and Ricky's big brown eyes were wide with shocked silence.

Deputy Reese stuck his hand out to Manny. "Wade Reese is the name. I'm deputy sheriff 'round here."

Manny remained in place, his arms never moving from the baby cradled within them. A few moments of utter quiet left Randi near panic and the deputy shuffling his feet uncomfortably.

Finally he turned back to Randi and pinned her with a dubious glare. "Who're they?"

Randi swallowed while she tried to think of some reasonable story. The more Wade stared at her, the more her mind went blank.

"Everything okay here, girl?" The deputy's hand hovered tentatively above the gun he wore holstered openly at his waist. Randi knew he'd never actually use the gun with her and the baby standing nearby, but the movement clearly spoke of Wade's growing suspicions.

She was frantic and trembling. Could she trust the dark and mysterious man she'd known only for about twelve hours? Or should she blurt out everything and take her chances with a deputy sheriff she'd known for most of her life? The answer seemed clear.

"Uh, Wade, this is Manny Sanchez...my fiancé." She could barely believe those words had really come from her own lips.

"Fiancé? Naw." The deputy's jaw dropped open.

He turned back and forth between the still-silent Manny and the ever more nervous Randi. "You're getting hitched? To him? Can't be. To my knowledge you don't even date. I don't believe it."

"Well, it's true." She figured Wade wouldn't be much of a test of her story-telling ability. He'd always been such a pushover for her. If she swore it was true, he'd believe.

Randi stepped around the bulky man in uniform and pulled the baby back into her arms. "And this is Manny's son, Ricky. Manny's a widower and I'm going to be Ricky's mama."

# Five

"**H**ave you gone totally nuts?" Manny whispered.

Randi continued to go through the motions of making coffee, even though her mind reeled with the reality of the lie she'd told. "We don't have to whisper. Wade's gone to check on Lewis Lee and Hannah. Their house is a quarter mile up the road."

"Don't you think he'll wonder why your neighbors have no idea you're engaged...have never met me...or have never even heard of me and Ricky?" He tapped his foot on the wood plank kitchen floor and jiggled the baby up and down in his arms.

Randi twisted around to glare at the man who'd suddenly become a pain in the neck. "I didn't think of that, all right?" She lit the stove and blew out the match. "I'll make up something. Don't worry. You'll be safe."

"It's not me I'm worried about, Randi. It's you...your reputation...your friends and family." The baby squirmed in his arms, so Manny set him down on the kitchen floor. "As soon as I can get hold of my boss and retrieve my bike, Ricky and I will be out of your house and out of your life forever. How are you going to explain that?"

"I told you...I'll think of a good story." She took a step toward the baby. The little boy grabbed hold of a chair leg and tried to pull himself up. "Besides, I was just trying to do what you asked and not give you away. Wade was becoming antsy about the situation. I don't usually have strange men and babies in my house. I had to say something. It was the first thing that popped into my head."

Ricky's efforts at standing failed after he'd raised himself about a half foot. He fell back on his bottom and let out a howl of fury. Randi reached for him just as the phone rang.

They looked at each other with stunned expressions. The phone lines were open. The implications of that fact hung in the air. Soon it would be time for Manny and Ricky to leave.

"You get the phone, I'll get the kid," Manny growled.

Randi pursed her lips, but swallowed back the smart-alec retort that bubbled in her throat. The man could be so infuriating. It was a good thing he would be leaving—wasn't it?

When she picked up the phone, Hannah's high, whining voice cracked through the static. "What's this we hear about you getting engaged, young lady? Just who is this man, anyway?" The prying questions spilled from the elderly woman's mouth faster than Randi could answer. "Is he from around here? Where'd you meet him?"

"Take it easy, Hannah. Everything is fine. I'll tell you all about it when I see you." Randi figured she needed a little more time to make up a good story for the old woman she'd known all her life. "The phones are working again, I see. Do you know if the water's gone down enough to get to the highway?" The change of topic bought her time.

"I don't know about the low-water bridge road, but the long way, past your stepfather's house, is open. Deputy Reese called the sheriff from here a few minutes ago.

"Seems like a man's body washed up a couple miles downstream from your property this morning. They don't know where the man came from, and the body was pretty beat up. The sheriff wanted his deputy to backtrack up the river to search out where the man went in the water."

Randi felt herself going weak. So—the driver was dead after all. She swallowed the nausea that threatened to end their conversation too soon.

Behind her Ricky cried out with a frustrated wail.

"What's that noise?" Hannah demanded. "Is that the baby Deputy Wade said was there? What's wrong with it?"

Randi tried to remind herself that Hannah was old and constantly in pain from arthritis and osteoporosis. She knew she had to cut the woman some serious slack— but honestly, she was sorely trying Randi's nerves this morning with all the questions.

"I'd better see to him, Hannah. Thanks for calling. I've got to go now." She hung up the phone and marched over to pull Ricky from Manny's arms.

"I take it that was your neighbor." Manny raised his voice to be heard over the baby's cries.

"Hannah is more than a neighbor. She and her husband, Lewis Lee, have lived on the Running C for longer than I have. When my daddy hired them, this place had dozens of hands. Daddy always said that Lewis Lee was the best ranch foreman in ten counties.''

"How many people work on the ranch now?''

"It's just Lewis Lee and me now. But since we sold off the herd there hasn't been all that much to keep us busy.''

"Uh-huh. I could tell that by the condition of your roof.''

While Randi soothed Ricky and offered him another bite of banana, she told Manny what Hannah had said about the dead man and the receding flood waters.

"Don't worry about the car or the body of the kidnapper.'' Manny looked as frustrated as Ricky had only minutes before. "My boss can smooth over any problem with the sheriff. Can I use your phone?''

Several hours later Manny's frustration had tripled. He stood in the muddy field with his boss, Reid Sorrels, Agent-in-Charge of the FBI's Operation Rock-a-Bye. They watched as a tow truck picked up his Harley, secured it in back and headed off to a shop in Willow Springs.

"The Harley dealer in Del Rio says it'll be some time before they can get the parts you need way out here. But it doesn't really matter anyhow. You won't be going anywhere for a while,'' Reid snarled. He flipped his service-issue, portable phone back into its holster on his belt and frowned at Manny.

"What's that supposed to mean?'' Manny's irritation rose as high as the humidity on this muggy autumn day.

"It means we need to find you a cover so you can stick around here.'' Reid drove his fingers through his hair, and for the first time in all the years he'd known him, Manny noticed silver splashing through his boss's brown strands. "The trail to the next level of baby stealers died with the scumbag who drowned. All we really know is he was headed to meet with his superior, and their meeting would've taken place at or near the Running C."

Reid propped his fists on his hips, glaring at Manny with one of his infamous black-eyed stares—guaranteed to rattle suspects and underlings alike.

Manny wasn't in the mood to be pushed, even by the one man he respected the most. "Now that you've informed the county sheriff about our operation, don't you think the trail will grow cold in a hurry, Reid? I imagine the entire county will hear about it within a few hours."

His Operation Rock-a-Bye superior waved off the objections. "I didn't mention the purpose of the mission, and the sheriff never saw you. Nobody but the tow-truck driver and that girl at the Running C know what you look like…and the driver didn't get a good look."

"The sheriff's deputy knows me," Manny protested. "But I guess he wouldn't connect me to you or the operation," he reluctantly conceded.

Manny was beginning to feel trapped, but he wasn't entirely sure by what—or who.

"I intend to inform the sheriff that we're moving the operation up-state," Reid continued. "His office will think we've moved on."

"Why don't we do just that…move Operation Rock-a-Bye up-state? We know this international gang's main man has to have political connections that allow the baby sellers to phony the paperwork so cleverly. Wouldn't it be smart just to move our sting toward the state capital?"

"Nope. Not yet. We need all the links in the chain. If we find the contact man in this area, we stand a better chance of following the trail to the real man in charge." Reid took a step out of the mud and scraped his boots against the gravel, apparently trying to dislodge a hunk of goo from his heels.

He continued talking. "Besides, I don't intend to let the man most responsible for the murder of that couple in Del Rio off scot-free. No way."

"You don't think it was an accident? It looked to me like the *coyote* who drowned just panicked in Del Rio and blew away the baby's parents when he thought he was being followed." At least, that's the way Manny had viewed the situation. And it still bothered him that his presence might have contributed to the murder of an innocent couple.

"This gang is too well trained and disciplined. For them, murder wouldn't happen in a panic. Even though the scum who pulled the trigger apparently panicked afterward and headed straight for his boss through a raging storm." Reid looked over at his undercover agent with a scowl. "Someone ordered those Mexican parents killed. I mean to give that couple a little justice. It's the least we can do for them—and for their baby."

Reid walked to his rental car and opened the back door. "I've brought you a new set of identity papers, a credit card, some cash and another satellite phone. I plan on using the Del Rio field office as a base of operations while we investigate the area. We have a few leads to follow up from there that might head in this direction. In the meantime, if you need anything just holler."

Reid bent to search inside the back seat. "The baby's safe, right?" he asked over his shoulder. "I'll fix it so you can keep him with you for a while longer if it'll help you with the operation.''

"I don't like using the kid.'' Manny folded his arms over his chest waiting for his boss to turn around. "You want him to be bait?''

"No, not at all.'' Reid jerked upright and faced him squarely. "I just meant he might add to your cover…give you a legitimate reason to ask about adoptions and stuff. You have any ideas about what kind of cover story would get you on the Running C the quickest?''

Manny groaned internally and wished he could be anywhere else right now, but unfortunately his duty was clear. "Yeah. I think I do. The main ranch house badly needs an extra pair of hands. There's probably enough work to keep a man busy there for the next twenty years.''

"Do you think you can get that girl-owner to hire you even with your gimpy shoulder?''

Having to stay on the ranch with Randi was definitely some kind of trap. A tender trap to be sure, but not one he would easily get out of in the end.

"The shoulder's just bruised. A couple days rest and it'll be fine.'' Manny stuffed the things Reid handed him into his pockets. "I'll keep the baby with me on the ranch…but only because I know I can guarantee his safety that way. Don't worry about the shoulder slowing me down. I have a special in with the owner anyhow.''

"Oh?''

With a quick nod, Manny swung and headed for the borrowed Suburban he'd parked up the road. Without turning around, he called back to his boss.

"Sure thing. I'm engaged to marry her.''

\* \* \*

Manny headed the truck toward the Running C by way of the back roads. In the last few hours, the waters had completely returned to their tame borders, leaving soggy debris cluttering up the landscape and causing him to creep along the highway. The stench of rotting vegetation assailed his nostrils, making him queasy. He rolled up the window and took shallow breaths.

He hadn't gone a half mile before he finally accepted that he and Ricky were going to be staying here indefinitely. When the full realization of that fact really sank in, he turned the truck around and headed toward Willow Springs.

A half hour later he found himself standing in line at a checkout stand at the local discount center. The heavy-set woman in front of him eyed his full basket.

"You just passing through town, son?" she asked.

"No, ma'am. We'll be here for some time."

Manny could see her mentally making assumptions about him from the various things in his basket—the main one being a child's car seat, designed to adjust for kids up to forty pounds.

"You and your wife staying with friends in the area?"

This was just the kind of nosy woman Manny normally loved to pump for information. Today he'd rather she mind her own business.

"No. It's just me and my son, and we're staying on a ranch near here."

The woman's eyebrows shot up. "I'm Nancy Kincade, and I know most of the people hereabouts. Which family you visiting?"

"We're staying on the Running C with Randi Cullen." Manny sighed, wishing once again he could close his eyes and transport himself a million miles away from this place.

When he blinked, the rather plain-looking woman suddenly scowled, bunching up her features and making her face look like sandpaper. "Just you and your son…alone at the main house with Randi? You a distant relative or something?"

Okay. The gossip was about to take root. He'd have to make up a story and stick to it in order to keep a handle on what was being told about them. He just had to pray Randi would go along with everything.

"Randi and I are engaged. I've come to help out around the ranch and be with her in her time of grief."

"Engaged? You and Randi Cullen?" The woman's face paled, and Manny noticed her grip tightening on the basket's handle.

"Yes'um." Why did everyone in town react so incredulously to a pretty young girl being engaged? Was it something about her that made them so astonished— or something about him? He suspected the latter.

"Does her stepfather know about this?"

Manny shook his head.

"Where you hail from, boy?"

"Uh, the Dallas area."

"And how do you know the Cullens?"

"They were old friends of my family." Ha! Not very likely in this lifetime, he thought.

"Hmm. Well, when are you two planning on tying the knot? It ain't fitting for a single man and woman to be alone on a ranch lessen they're married." The woman hitched up her flower-print dress and glared at him. "There's some folks round these parts that would gossip, and I'm sure you wouldn't want unkind things said about your future wife."

"We're not alone at the main house." He nodded toward the basket mostly full of baby things. "My son is with us."

"You a divorced man, boy?"

"My name is Manny Sanchez, ma'am. And I'm a widower."

That seemed to take some of the steam out of her. What a perfect cover story this made! Every woman in town would now feel sorry for him and the baby. He waited a moment while the fuss-budget in front of him got the required sympathetic look in her eyes.

She did, but it was tempered with wariness. "Well now, that's purely a shame, but you still can't be staying out there for long. It just ain't right."

"You...you...decided what?" Randi was flabbergasted.

She patted Ricky's diapered bottom, and smiled at how it stuck straight up in the air as he lay sleeping on his knees and tummy in the basket. But the smile fled as she turned to shake her head at the dark and daring man standing so calmly in her kitchen.

Manny, arms folded across his chest, stared at her through half-closed eyes that saw straight to her soul.

"I've changed my mind," he said in a low voice. "I want Ricky and me to stay on here with you for a while. I'll be happy to help out around the ranch and even pay for room and board if you'll let us stay."

She waved off the suggestion, but had to turn away from the sight of the new black T-shirt tightly encompassing his muscular chest. "But I thought you needed to leave. I...I thought you wanted to be on your way as soon as possible?"

"Well, *I've* been thinking about your little white lie to the deputy. Pretending we're engaged and getting you out of your jam seems like the least I can do for helping me with Ricky and for taking us in out of the storm."

Of all the arrogant, self-centered, self-righteous idiots on earth, this guy really took the cake, she fumed.

"I certainly do not need that kind of help. I told you I could take care of it." She spun to look him in the eyes.

Actually the help she really needed was around the ranch and around her heart. She felt needy and dumb and tried desperately not to let him notice.

Manny stepped closer to her and studied her. "Randi," he whispered.

He reached one hand to touch her, but halted it in midair, inches away from contact with her arm. "Let me help. Let Ricky and me stay for a while. I—" he cleared his throat "—we need you."

Her knees began to shake. Did he just say what she thought he'd said? Suddenly she found her eyes fixed on his hand, still hovering above her skin. All she could think of was having his hands on her again—and of the kiss they'd shared last night.

She closed her eyes and felt herself leaning forward toward him—as if he were the sun and she a morning glory desperate to open and begin to really live.

The silence was deafening. A whisper of movement and she could swear he'd moved closer to her still. Touching but not touching. Hungering but holding the feast in check.

When she opened her eyes, she found he'd stepped back and, with a strange look in his eyes, stood patiently holding a small plastic bag in his hand.

"I bought this for you in town." He shoved the bag at her and glanced away. "I figured it would make the whole thing appear more legit."

Still shaking slightly, Randi took the bag from his hand and opened it. Inside, some small article lay nestled within layers of tissue paper.

"It isn't worth much," he interjected, as she slowly unfolded the crisp, crackling tissue. "But it looked pretty realistic."

"A diamond engagement ring?" She held the gold-banded gem in her palm and raised her head, trying to find some answer in his eyes. What was he telling her? What was he really asking?

Manny's expression was stern and hard. "Not a diamond. It's just a glass ring." He narrowed his eyebrows. "A fake ring for a pretend engagement. My boss wants me to stick around the Running C. He wants me to use you and Ricky to find the kidnapper's contact man."

She knew a scarlet flush of embarrassment rushed up her throat and covered her face. How foolish and naive must she be, for heaven's sake? Of course this was part of his job and definitely not a declaration of love.

"Oh. I see."

She'd known for years that she was not the kind of woman to inspire any great passion. But she wanted it so badly she'd obviously turned into some kind of basket case—desperate to have someone who would really care about her and never leave her behind.

She turned her back to him so he couldn't see the tears threatening to spill from her eyes.

*Just glass tears.* Fake tears for a pretend love, she echoed to herself. She bit down on her lip to cover the hurt inside.

"Oh, Randi. I'm so sorry. I didn't mean to trick you. Or to…hurt you," he murmured. "I never thought… Look, I'll tell my boss it's no good. We'll just have to think of some other way to find the man who ordered the murder of Ricky's parents.''

His words penetrated the haze of her pain. There were so many good reasons to go along with the story. Manny had a job to do. A worthwhile job that meant protection for the community and justice for Ricky.

Besides, she'd been foolish enough to start the whole darned mess when she'd blurted out that stupid phony engagement story in a moment of panic. Going ahead with it would give her time to come up with a better story for her neighbors and friends.

Her final reason was that going along with the story would keep Manny and Ricky on the ranch. Close to her. Maybe with a little more time she could find out what having a man and a family of her own would be like—even if it was only a temporary situation.

She steadied herself by swallowing hard. ''I'll be happy to have you stay on the ranch and tell everyone we're engaged, Mr. Sanchez.''

She slipped the ring on her finger and turned to face her pretend fiancé intending to paste a fake smile on her face. And that's when a very real feeling thudded in her heart. It was an ache of longing so strong it nearly knocked her down.

*Dear God.* How was she ever going to pull this off and not be destroyed in the process?

# Six

When Lewis Lee stopped by later that afternoon, Randi nearly panicked once again. She wondered how he and Manny would get along and whether Lewis Lee, the friend who'd known her longer than she could remember, would buy her story.

She really hadn't had a chance to think up a plausible explanation for why she hadn't mentioned Manny and the baby to anyone. Randi had wanted to think it through later—after Manny had finished his mission and left the ranch. Torn between wanting to keep him here and not wanting to lie to her friends, she had hoped beyond hope that maybe she could just slide through this whole thing.

"So, you've gone and gotten yourself a man, huh, kitten?" Lewis Lee eyed Manny suspiciously when she'd introduced them, but he did manage to shake the younger man's hand.

"Where'd you two meet up?" Lewis Lee asked her.

Randi looked to Manny for help, but the look on his face made it clear the story would be up to her. "Uh, remember right after Mom died when I took some of her things up to Aunt Emily in Waco? It was then." She cast another nervous glance behind her to Manny, but found no emotion or help in those silent, caramel-colored eyes.

Lewis Lee nodded, turning to face Manny head-on. Randi held her breath, waiting for the questions or the lecture she was sure would be coming from this man who'd been the closest thing to a father that she'd had since her own had passed away. She hated lying to him, but this whole thing had taken on a life of its own.

"You ride, son?"

Manny straightened his shoulders, adjusted the baby against his chest and took a step forward. "I figure I can keep up with you, old man."

A couple of moments of strained silence had Randi jumping inside her skin, but she stayed quiet.

Lewis Lee broke the stalemate. "You gonna lie around here all day, or you figure you can spare the time to look over the spread you'll be marrying into?"

"Wait just a minute, Lewis Lee," Randi blurted. "*If* we get married, he won't be marrying the ranch, he'll be marrying me. And he isn't lying around. His shoulder is injured." She took Ricky from Manny's arms.

Neither man paid her any heed, but continued to stare each other down as if they were about to have a gunfight in the street. Without another word Manny walked over to the peg where he'd hung his new Resistol work hat, adjusted it low on his forehead and opened the back door.

"Don't wait dinner on me, Randi. This might take a while," he said soberly.

The two men went off, leaving her wondering what they might do or say to each other. She could scarcely believe that Lewis Lee had bought their story so easily. True enough the man seldom had much to say, but Randi was astonished at his lack of questions. She knew his wife would be another story, and she hoped she could put off that little inquisition for as long as possible. Maybe before then, Manny and Ricky would be gone and she could just say she couldn't bear to talk about it. Hmm…

When Manny rode off with Lewis Lee to get a look at the ranch, he'd expected a lecture about the indecency of staying with Randi. But the lecture he received instead was about not hurting the young woman and about the pride and glory that used to belong to the Running C.

Manny could see for himself the potential and the history of the place. It was a real shame not to use the land as a cattle ranch, the way her ancestors intended. But without a family to back her, Randi's days on this ranch appeared to be numbered.

In the long haul, there wasn't anything that Manny could do one way or the other to stop it. He wouldn't even be here long enough to slow the process down much. That was one hurt he was powerless to save her from.

It was a shame that his own family hadn't had a community where they belonged, and that his reputation had always been one to live down instead of one to uphold. But he knew how much a reputation must mean to her. After the ranch was gone, that was all she'd have left. He also realized how hard it would be for her to hold her head up against the gossip and lies once he'd headed on to a new assignment.

For the next couple of days, Manny left the house in silence, riding off at dawn with Lewis Lee and doing as many chores as his bum shoulder would allow.

Randi seemed happy to be taking care of Ricky. She'd said she didn't mind a bit telling her boss a few fibs so she could stay home and not have to face the whole town with her made-up story.

This morning, as he'd tried to sneak down the stairs before it got light, he'd found her sitting in front of a mirror, brushing her hair. It was such a feminine and soft vision, he'd found it hard to keep on moving.

"Morning," he mumbled.

"Oh, good morning." She turned to him and beamed. "You want me to fix you breakfast? Ricky won't be up for a little while yet."

He shook his head and again tried to move past the doorway, but his boots glued themselves to the carpet.

"Where's the sling we made up for your arm?" she asked.

"The shoulder's better. I don't need it anymore. It's time I started earning my keep around here."

"You really don't have to work on the ranch, you know," she insisted. "Besides, you already have a job. Lewis Lee and I can handle things on the ranch like always."

He figured he'd better go to work. Otherwise, he could easily see himself hanging around, getting to know the fascinating woman who'd taken them in—and playing house with her and the baby all day.

"I can do both jobs at the same time, sugar. And it's time I got to them." He forced himself down the stairs and away from temptation.

Randi threw her brush down on the dresser with a thump. A couple more days of this forced politeness and starched correctness might really be the end of her. She'd imagined that living with Manny and getting close to him would break her heart after he'd gone, but she'd found living in the same house and *not* being close to him was much worse.

In the past forty-eight hours, instead of too much togetherness, he'd said no more than a dozen words to her—except those concerning Ricky. At night Manny slept in her parents' old bedroom and she kept the baby in her room, in a crib Manny bought in Willow Springs. In the evenings he cooked, cleaned and helped with Ricky—mostly in silence.

Thoughts of his job, his life before this, and what he really wanted from her had turned her as jittery as a barn mouse stealing a horse's feed. Wondering and daydreaming had been all she could do, however, because she couldn't bring herself to demand any answers from him. Now she made a vow to herself to find a way.

She wanted them to become close, both emotionally and physically, before she lost her chance forever. How would they ever become friends, let alone lovers, if he never paid any attention to her?

A few long hours later Randi stepped out into the crystal-clear, late-fall sunshine. She dragged the wash basket behind her, ready to hang the baby's clothes on the line while Ricky napped. She'd heard Manny on the roof a while ago and hoped to catch a glimpse of him.

As she began her chore, her dear friend, Marian Baker, drove into the yard and got out of her ten-year-old Pontiac with a smile on her face.

"Randi, we've missed you." Marian hugged her tightly.

Marian, five or six years older than Randi, was the town's spinster librarian. She also had a kind spirit and was as close as Randi would ever get to a best friend. Today she'd dressed in a sophisticated skirt and blouse with an animal pattern, and Randi thought she appeared a bit on edge.

"Thanks." Randi backed out of Marian's embrace and searched the roof for any sign of Manny.

Marian pushed a wisp of auburn-colored hair behind her ear and followed Randi's gaze. "Where is he?" she whispered.

"You mean Manny?"

"Is that his name? All I heard was that he's a handsome and brooding hunk. I've been dying to meet him and see for myself."

The man in question suddenly appeared from around the corner of the house. He looked so dangerous and so darkly gorgeous both women gasped at the sight. A second later they broke into a childish giggle at their own silliness, but as he came closer they froze, mouths gaping open.

His brand-new jeans were covered in sawdust and clung to him like they were wet, exposing every muscle and bulge. He'd removed his shirt and was using it at the moment to mop the sweat from his forehead. The action caused his biceps to expand and contract and gave Randi the exact same feelings deep in her gut.

"My God. His arms are as big around as my thighs," Marian gushed.

The tangled, black hair on his chest glistened like a thousand diamond chips in the sunlight. It lay matted against his skin and Randi noticed the swirls seemed to all be pointing in the same direction—downward across that exquisite expanse of rippling muscle toward his belly button and the waistband of his jeans. Those same jeans that were now riding seductively low on his hips.

Whew, baby. Randi had to pinch herself to keep from imagining where exactly that point of hair might stop.

"Yep. A hunk if I ever saw one," Marian declared.

Randi found the presence of mind to usher all of them out of the sun and into the kitchen for a drink of lemonade.

After introductions and the same explanations they'd given to Lewis Lee, Randi figured Marian would be harder to convince. A few minutes later Manny went to check on Ricky, leaving the two women in an awkward silence.

"Do you love him? Does he make you happy?" Marian finally demanded.

What questions! Those weren't ones she'd thought through. In the back of her mind, Randi wondered if she would ever truly know the first thing about love or happiness, but she managed to nod in the affirmative to her friend.

"Why didn't you tell me about him before?"

Now *that* was a question for which Randi had prepared an answer. "I didn't think our relationship was serious. His showing up here and proposing took me by surprise."

"When are y'all getting married?"

"We don't have plans yet," Randi answered quickly.

"What do you know about him? What does he do for a living?"

"I know enough," Randi hedged. "Right now he's between jobs, but he's volunteered to help out on the ranch."

Marian shot a wary glance down the hall where Manny had disappeared and, turning back to Randi, she puckered her mouth for a second. "I don't mean to be nosy...or preachy, but I've always felt a bit protective of you, sweetie. The whole town's talking about you two. He shouldn't be staying here."

She took Randi's hands in her own. Marian must have felt the new addition to her friend's left hand because she stared at the ring as if it was a rattler. She didn't mention it, though, just continued speaking directly to Randi.

"You know I care about you, don't you?" she asked her younger friend.

"Of course."

"Then believe that I only want what's best for you. A single woman simply cannot be living out here on the ranch alone with a man...engaged or not. What will your stepfather say when he finds out? You know he doesn't much care for...uh...that he's so prejudiced against—"

Randi drew her head back and tried to pull away. Marian held her fast with a gentle tug just as Manny appeared in the doorway.

"All right. Forget I mentioned Frank Riley," Marian conceded. "But this is a small town, my friend. People talk. Some people would be glad to find a reason to bring shame and trouble to anyone from a family as well-known and respected as yours. It's just jealousy, I know, but it'll bite you if you let it get out of control."

Manny stood in the hallway listening to the woman with the sweet face and the plain words. He'd been a little anxious about her at the beginning. Everyone in town was a suspect until he discovered otherwise, but she seemed so genuinely concerned for Randi's welfare that his gut told him she would turn out to be simply a friend.

The more he heard of Marian's words, the more he realized what a tenuous position he'd carelessly let Randi step into. When this Operation Rock-a-Bye mission was over and the man he sought was brought down, he could take Ricky to safety and walk away—they would go on with their lives and never look back. But what about Randi? She had to stay here and be part of the community where she'd been raised, where her family had a name and a reputation to uphold.

He decided he couldn't go through with the pretense. He'd call Reid and tell him he had to find a way to get them out of this stupid mess—and soon.

"Marry me." Manny heard himself speak the words, but couldn't believe they really came from his mouth.

Randi had put Ricky to bed while Manny washed the dinner dishes. After the baby fell asleep, she'd dried the dishes, Manny had stacked and now, at this late hour, he'd decided to try sorting out a good plan of action for them.

Reid hadn't been particularly helpful this afternoon when Manny asked for assistance in finding a new cover story. When his boss suggested he actually marry Randi, it seemed downright asinine. Yet here he was proposing that very thing.

"Excuse me?" Randi dropped the dish towel and her eyes widened, turning from their normally sexy green into a dark honey color.

He almost lost his train of thought by staring at the fascinating colors in her eyes, wondering if they would get that same color when she was in the throes of passion. He clamped down on his emotions, figuring they both had a lot more to lose than just their train of thought.

"In name only, of course." He didn't want to hedge, but he had to make her fully understand his position. "I realize you don't really know me, but hear me out before you make any snap judgments about our situation, will you?''

Since he'd been there, each time that he'd gone into town trying to get a line on the baby smugglers, the townsfolk had turned their backs on him. Oh, sure, most of the women stared and giggled when he walked by, but no one seemed willing to have any kind of real conversation.

Apparently, just because he and Randi were engaged didn't mean that he was going to be accepted. Between his Mexican-American heritage and Willow Springs's old-fashioned moral code, he and Randi would be social outcasts as long as he was staying with her.

Manny finally figured that he could make better headway with the Mexican-American farmhands at nearby ranches, and he had indeed made a few contacts with them. But both he and Reid had come to the conclusion that the smugglers' contact man here had to be more influential than the ranch hands could possibly be. In fact, their man was probably somehow connected to the law around here. That made everything more difficult.

Manny knew he must be able to ask questions of everyone, and as of right now, about half the town wouldn't even talk to him—or to Randi for that matter.

Randi refolded the dish towel and set it aside. Taking a deep breath, she leaned against the countertop and waited silently for Manny to speak.

She'd pulled her hair back into a makeshift braid tonight. Little wisps of radiant, ash-blond hair framed her face and made her look like she'd stepped through a thousand gossamer spider webs. He was certain she wasn't trying to look sexy, but that's all Manny could think when he saw her standing there in the glow of the dim kitchen light.

Back to the business at hand, he scolded himself.

"Getting married would be a good way to defuse the gossip around town and keep your reputation intact."

Her eyes were pale green again and seemed to stare right through him with no reaction to his words. What could he say to make her understand?

Maybe the truth would make a difference.

"Randi, the cover isn't working for me this way. Instead of enabling me to get close to your friends and neighbors, my living here has caused a split between them and you...leaving me out in the cold. I need to be inside the community...not isolated from it."

She blinked and he figured maybe he was making an impression after all.

"We could get a judge to perform the ceremony, and after I capture our man, my boss could easily get us an annulment. It would be like it never happened...except your friends and neighbors will accept both of us as a married couple...me especially."

"You think I'd be better off afterward as a divorcee rather than as a woman who'd lived in sin?" she asked.

He felt an odd tingle on the back of his neck when she mentioned the word *sin*. He paused, clamping down on the immediate images and urgent needs suddenly pounding inside him, and tried to ignore the beads of sweat forming in the small of his back.

"We wouldn't be divorced," he argued at last. "An annulment is more like it never happened."

"Is that what my friends would think? That the marriage never happened?"

He saw it now. The slight curl at the corner of her lips. The twinkle in her eyes. The overall smirk on her face that said she was putting him on.

"What do you want from me, sugar?" He laughed with an exasperated shake of his head.

Randi wished she knew what she wanted from him. When he'd mentioned marriage, an uncomfortable sensation skidded down her spine, sending jolts of heat straight to her belly. The feeling was odd but enticing. A new kind of awareness overtook her mind, and an odd image, one without substance, raised goose bumps on her skin.

She found she had to close her eyes, fighting to keep her mind clear and still sound coherent at the same time.

"I…" He was close enough that when she took a deep breath she inhaled him.

His scent was a combination of dish soap, coffee and an elusive smell that seemed to belong just to him. At once, that unnamed scent both terrified and comforted her. And it seemed very much like something she'd been waiting for all her life.

She had to resist rolling her eyes at her own foolishness. She had a feeling she was about to step off the edge of a cliff. One where she'd never been before and surely didn't belong.

"Okay. I'll marry you," she answered quickly, before she could think it through enough to see how dumb a move this might really be.

When he chuckled again, it was low, rich and sensual. Not only rich, but smooth and soft like fine, cut velvet.

"Wait a minute." Manny dug into his boot and pulled free a thin plastic case.

"Before you agree to marry someone, you should at least check out his credentials. I want you to know that I'm on the level." He flipped open the case and handed it to her.

Immediately, Randi saw the words: Federal Bureau of Investigation. An FBI agent? Omigosh!

Handing him back the case, she said, "I never doubted you were on the level."

She felt herself begin to tremble and clasped her arms over her chest to keep him from seeing her nervousness. The things his mere voice could do to her insides scared and confused her.

Manny placed his broad hands on her shoulders, pinning her with a tender grip and causing her to wish she could squirm. But she held herself still.

"Thank you," he murmured.

His eyes turned the color of creamed coffee as they searched hers. She pulled her lower lip into her mouth trying to clear her head, but all she could think about was the way his ebony hair fell over his forehead in deep, textured strands. She very much wanted to touch it, so she jammed her hands into the back pockets of her jeans.

"I intend to do everything in my power to see that you don't get hurt from any of this, darlin'."

When his gaze fell on her mouth, she had an overpowering urge to lick her lips. As her tongue slid out, the look in his eyes quickly changed to something dark and dangerous. His hands slid off her shoulders, and he took a step back.

"I think it will be for the best if we try to remember that this is an assignment." He quickly crammed his hands into his own jeans pockets, making her wonder if he'd felt the same way she had. "We won't be playing house for real. I won't expect you to do anything that even remotely resembles wifely duties."

She stared at his lean, hardened features as that gut-level feeling she still didn't recognize pushed her to move silently toward him. He took one more hesitating step backward, and she realized she'd been wrong. He didn't feel the same way at all—foolish girl.

"Randi, I've been through too much heartache in my life. I'm afraid I'm not a very nice person. I've had to do some things for the sake of the job that I'm not proud of. You don't want to become involved with the real Manuel Sanchez."

She'd stopped where she was but never said a word, merely stood there looking soft and vulnerable. His legs felt as if they were stuck in quicksand. He needed to get the heck away from her—badly. But a ferocious desire to take her in his arms kept him suspended between good sense and paradise.

When she'd sucked on her lower lip, he experienced an internal demand like no other he'd ever known. Some inner voice pushed him to protect her. To lay down his life for this woman he barely knew. To make her understand how really dangerous any relationship with him might be.

Before he reconciled that need, she'd let go of her lip and it glistened with moisture. The protective instinct he'd felt gave way to a more basic urge. The tip of her pink tongue had peeked out between her lips, sending leaping life to his already hardened manhood.

He couldn't let her become involved with him. Just because they were going to be married didn't mean that they had to get close to each other. He could help her with her ranch, and she could help him with Ricky while he searched for the bad guy. Simple. Neat. All business.

He couldn't touch her. Not even for a moment. It would be easier to walk away.

Before that rational thought could extinguish his needs, she was in his arms. She laid her head on his chest and he leaned his cheek against her hair. So soft. So erotic.

"What are you doing?" he whispered into the silky wisps. "Have some good sense and run away," he said, as much to himself as to her.

She pulled her head back to look at him. The intensity and longing he saw in her eyes caused a fervent craving to rise up in him, rushing past all his good arguments against getting close to her.

"I'm not running. I want…"

Whether she'd wanted him to stop or whether she'd wanted him to go on, he would never know because suddenly his hunger weakened whatever resolve he had left. He was destined to taste her again. Just one more time.

He pressed his lips to hers, trying to be as gentle as the flaming need inside him would allow. She was young and inexperienced. Even in his steamy zeal, he knew he would frighten her if he came on too strong.

The conflict inside him grew as he nipped at her bottom lip. This was so wrong for her. But it felt so right.

Randi felt her lips quiver, and opened them against his tongue's tender assault. When he tentatively explored her mouth, her tongue found his and she leaned into his chest, moaning deep in her throat.

All sense, all reason, all good intentions had apparently fled.

Before she could think through what he was doing, his hands slid under her T-shirt and found the sensitive skin of her rib cage. She stopped breathing.

They'd managed to back themselves into the counter. As she pressed herself against him, she noticed the peaks of her breasts were hard—aching for his touch. He pushed his groin against hers and she felt his growing need.

That she could do that sort of thing to a man was an intoxicating thought—full of promise. He pulled his lips away from hers, and began kissing his way down her neck.

His hands slid up her swollen breasts. He cupped them and moved to cover the peaks. She gasped and began panting.

He reached for the edge of her T-shirt when out of the haze she thought she heard a baby's wail. He must have heard it, too, because his head came up to listen. With their sudden stillness, she heard nothing except the sounds of the night beyond the kitchen window. But Manny dropped his hands and turned to look down at her.

"Did I do something wrong?" she asked. "Don't stop, please."

He'd hesitated and Randi figured her lack of experience must have been why. Clumsy inexperience was about to ruin her life.

"Look. Uh…" she stuttered.

She'd wanted this moment to be so right. "The thing is…I'm a virgin…but I'm a fast learner and I swear I'll do better if you'll please just bear—"

# Seven

"S-s-stop," Manny sputtered. "I don't want to know any more."

He gasped, wondering if his lack of air could still be reversed by taking a breath or if he might actually choke to death. Now, if he could just remember how to breathe...

"Are you okay?" Randi asked in an innocent tone. "Can I get you some water?"

A virgin, for cripe's sake. He should've figured. What had come over him to kiss her the way he had? Out of an entire lifetime full of jackass moves, this had to be the most stupid one he'd ever made.

"No. I don't want you to do anything." He groaned as he moved to the sink.

She opened a cupboard and handed him a glass.

"How old are you?" He filled the glass and took a slug.

"Twenty-four." Randi looked devastated.

"Great. Just what I need. I'm supposed to find a guy who's responsible for the murder of at least two people and I'm saddled with a baby and a twenty-four-year-old virgin."

Her confession must have short-circuited his brain because all he wanted, all he could think about, was kissing her again.

A lot was at stake here, several people's lives hung on his actions, and instead of sharp wit and sure plans, Manny's mind was fuzzy-headed and befuddled. *Damn it.*

"Manny?"

His name rolled off her tongue with that slight West Texas accent, and he realized it was the first time she'd called him by name.

He took another swallow of water and reined in whatever stray emotions were bouncing around in his brain. "I'm ten years older than you, and I'm supposed to know better than to let anything like this happen while I have to concentrate on an assignment." He set the glass down and tentatively grasped her shoulders, looking her straight in the eyes.

"Number one—you don't tell a man in the middle of a kiss that you're a...well, uh, not experienced."

"When are you supposed to give someone that kind of information?"

"When you're engaged." He could hear himself shouting and fought to calm his tone.

"But..." She raised her left hand and pointed at the glass ring on her finger. "I thought we were."

He shook his head, bit down on the urge to roar and pinned her with his best scowl. "You know what I'm

# Play the LUCKY Carnival Wheel Game...

GET YOUR 3 GIFTS FREE !

PLAY FOR FREE ! NO PURCHASE NECESSARY !

# HOW TO PLAY:

1. With a coin, carefully scratch off the 3 gold areas on your Lucky Carnival Wheel. By doing so you have qualified to receive everything revealed—2 FREE books and a surprise gift—ABSOLUTELY FREE!

2. Send back this card and you'll receive 2 brand-new Silhouette Desire® novels. These books have a cover price of $4.25 each in the U.S. and $4.99 each in Canada, but they are yours ABSOLUTELY FREE.

3. There's no catch! You're under no obligation to buy anything. We charge nothing—ZERO—for your first shipment. And you don't have to make any minimum number of purchases—not even one!

4. The fact is thousands of readers enjoy receiving books by mail from the Silhouette Reader Service™. They enjoy the convenience of home delivery...they like getting the best new novels at discount prices, BEFORE they're available in stores... and they love their *Heart to Heart* subscriber newsletter featuring author news, horoscopes, recipes, book reviews and much more!

5. We hope that after receiving your free books you'll want to remain a subscriber. But the choice is yours—to continue or cancel, any time at all! So why not take us up on our invitation, with no risk of any kind. You'll be glad you did!

**A surprise gift**

# FREE

**We can't tell you what it is...but we're sure you'll like it! A**

# FREE GIFT!

**just for playing LUCKY CARNIVAL WHEEL!**

Visit us online at
www.eHarlequin.com

talking about. You're supposed to wait for love, damn it!''

"Oh." She looked so timid and stung, he had the urge to cuddle her up and kiss her fears away.

"But I thought men didn't equate love with sex. I might not ever be loved in my lifetime. But once before I die, I want to find out what the big deal is about the other."

*Dios mio!* Manny wanted to crawl in a hole and disappear. How did he ever get into this conversation? He had no choice now but to see it through to the end; otherwise, he'd be the worst kind of coward.

"In the second place," he went on, trying to ignore her last remarks. "Well...there is no second place, but you can't just go around springing surprises like that on people."

A light shudder rumbled through her, and he had to release her shoulders before he did something even more stupid than he already had. "What's wrong with all the boys around here that are your age? Why hasn't one of them stamped a brand on you by now?"

"I guess it's because they've never had the chance...or they didn't want to get involved. My mother took up the bulk of my time, and my stepfather intimidated everyone else who might have gotten past that. I think they were afraid he'd sue them."

"But surely you've dated. Didn't those guys try a few things?"

This *was* a trap. The trap from hell. He didn't want to think about some local jerk trying anything with her. It made him mad just to ask about such a thing.

"Actually...I've never been on a real date."

"What? I don't believe you. What about that Deputy

Wade fellow? The way he looked at you, I thought for sure you two had been an item once upon a time.''

"Wade? No. I've known him all my life, but he's never asked me to go out.''

Deep down Randi didn't want to admit these kinds of things, especially not to the devastatingly gorgeous man who'd been living in her house. The look in his eyes when she'd first said she was a virgin told the whole story.

She'd read somewhere that men preferred women who knew how to please. Obviously, that book had been right. Manny's ardor cooled so fast her head swam when she'd admitted the truth.

But she could learn, couldn't she? In fact, she was determined to learn.

"I'm afraid I'm not the kind of woman men find attractive or sexy.''

"Randi.'' His voice seemed to lower two octaves as he picked up her hand. "You are one of the most beautiful women I've ever met. And believe me, I've met quite a few in my time. Any man in his right mind would find you irresistible.''

She could feel herself blush again and wished for a tan to hide her feelings. But, of course, she never tanned—she only burned. Her whole life was one impossible wish after another.

"But I'm just not particularly attractive to *you,* is that it?''

He laughed in that low, sexy way of his, setting her entire body on edge. "Ah...guess I asked for that. I never said I was in my right mind, did I?''

Oh, brother! She'd put her foot in her mouth that time.

He brought her hand to his lips, lightly nibbling and making her think of tiny feathers skimming across her skin. "It isn't you, sugar. It's me. You're too much of a distraction. I have a job to do."

"But we'll be *married*."

"We're being married to make my cover seem more realistic. It's part of my job...period. Wait for love, sweet Randi. Don't sell yourself short."

Short—my foot, she fumed, silently. She was absolutely positive that a smart woman could seduce any man who thought she was "irresistible"—no matter what the circumstances. She'd read about it often enough in books, hadn't she?

Well, if other women could figure out how to do it, so could she. She'd learned how to manage livestock through books. She'd learned to do the accounts and to be a nurse and physical therapist for her mother from books. This would be just one more thing to learn.

Three days later Marian stopped by the ranch with another special order of books for Randi.

"Whew! When are you going to have that road graded?" Marian complained. "The bumps are a disaster. I nearly split my lip when I hit my head on the roof of the car."

"Manny plans on borrowing a grader and seeing to the road tomorrow."

"He can do that? That's some man you've got there."

Randi heard the unspoken question in her friend's voice. "Yeah, I know. What does a guy like that see in me?" She sighed and took a breath. "That's what you're thinking, isn't it?"

"No. Not at all. It's just..." Marian dumped her armload of books on the kitchen table and went to soothe Ricky, who had dropped a toy. "He made this playpen for his son, too, didn't he?"

"Yes, but..."

Marian turned, a bittersweet expression on her face. "Oh, Randi, I don't want to see you get hurt. I can tell you really care about this guy and his baby. Are you sure his intentions are the best?"

"I know what you're saying, Marian. You think Manny's marrying me just to provide a mother for Ricky." Randi turned to pick up the toy. "It's not like that exactly. But what if it was? So what? When is a person like me ever going to get a chance at happiness again?"

"Life is not the same as in your books, sweetie. Don't sell yourself short. You have a lot to offer any man."

Randi bit her tongue to keep from screaming. Why was everyone all of a sudden so concerned about her "selling" herself? That just wasn't fair. So far in her life, she hadn't even been able to *give* herself away. If helping the FBI and stealing a little happiness at the same time was selling out—so be it. It's my life, dang it.

At Randi's silence, Marian shrugged her shoulders and began absently fingering the books she'd dropped on the table. "Manny's not around, is he?"

Randi shook her head. "He's out helping Lewis Lee bale the last of the fall hay."

"Good. I don't suppose you'd want him to see these books you asked me to order." Marian pulled the top two books off the stack and read from their covers. "*A Guide to Revitalizing Your Sex Life. How to Make a Man Beg*. I didn't even know the library system carried such titles."

Randi felt herself turning scarlet. "Thanks for bringing these out. Uh...no one saw them, did they?"

"No. Your secret is safe with me." Marian hesitated,

setting the books back on the table. "But, sweetie, why on earth would you think you needed such information? I can't imagine that a man's man like Manny would need any coaxing. Just because he wants to wait until his wedding night to…"

Randi shook her head so hard she thought she might've sprained her neck. "I really don't want to talk about this. It's too…personal." She grabbed the stack of books and jammed them into the back of a cabinet. "Please believe me. I know what I'm doing."

She wished she could explain all of this to Marian. It would be nice to talk to someone about the many changes in her life. But if she even *hinted* at the real reason she and Manny were getting married it might cost him his job—or maybe his life.

"All right. Have it your way." Marian lifted Ricky from his playpen. "I have that old dress you wanted altered in my trunk. Kimmi Sue asked me to bring it by. That the one you plan on wearing to the wedding? It belonged to your mother, didn't it?"

"My mother wore the dress on her wedding day, but it belonged to my great-grandmother originally."

"Pee-yew! This kid needs a change of diaper." Marian scrunched up her nose and held Ricky out at arm's length.

Randi had to suppress her laughter at her friend's discomfort. She took the baby and laid him down on the makeshift changing table she'd fashioned on a counter.

"Really, Marian, you'd think you'd never been around babies before."

"Oh, I have. I come from a family of six kids, remember. I just don't need to get that close to a dirty one."

Randi chuckled. "You're still planning on standing up with me at the wedding this weekend, aren't you?"

"Of course. But I don't understand why you two have to rush into this thing. What's wrong with getting married in the church and inviting a few more friends? If it's the money, I know we'd all pitch in for..."

Randi held up one free hand to stop her friend's offer. "No, thanks. It isn't a matter of money." She finished sticking the tabs on the disposable diaper Manny had bought for Ricky and picked him up. "We want to get married as soon as possible. That's all there is to it."

Marian's eyes narrowed slightly. "If Manny is so anxious to be married to you, then why the need for all that, uh, information?" She waved her arm toward the cabinet containing the secret books.

"Believe me, Marian, I'd love to talk to you about this sometime, but I'm just so busy today."

She hated having to lie to her best friend about her relationship to Manny. For his sake she'd done it, but she refused to make things any worse by trying to make up a story about why she needed the books.

"Okay. I get the hint. I'm going." Marian turned to head out the back door. "Go ahead and read the books if it makes you feel better, hon, but I have a feeling that most of what you'll need will come naturally. And I can't imagine that Manny will require even the slightest bit of convincing...or tutoring."

At three in the afternoon on the following Saturday, Randi stood in the ladies' room at the Uvalde County Courthouse, looking in a mirror while Marian tried to attach a corsage to her dress.

"Stand still, please. I don't want to pin these beautiful white roses to your skin." Marian took a step backward to scrutinize the placement of the corsage at Randi's waist. "It was certainly a lovely gesture for Manny to buy you these flowers. If you'd just have let me, I'd have bought you a bouquet and thrown you one heck of a reception, as well."

Randi tsked her friend. "I told you we didn't want a fuss."

"Maybe not, but that dress looks spectacular on you and more people should be able to get a gander at how great you look. This is your special day."

Randi looked down at herself in the mirror. She did look rather special today. The dress her great-grandmother had sewn for her own wedding looked fresh and new. The pearl-colored satin lining peeked through a barely beige lace overdress. To update it, she'd had the seamstress hem it to midcalf and shorten the sleeves to three-quarter length.

She'd left the square-cut bodice alone, and now in the mirror Randi knew that had been the right decision. The cut showed off a cleavage she hadn't even been sure she possessed. Grateful she could squeeze into the dress without major alterations, she was amazed and proud that Great-Grandmother Sarah must have been just about her size.

All this thinking about the dress reminded Randi of what she'd found carefully wrapped in tissue and lying securely under the wedding dress in the old chest. That package had been quite a surprise. Her mother, the optimist, had placed a brand-new white negligee, two pair of see-through white stockings and a white lace garter belt in the hope chest with a note to Randi about the grandchildren she "hoped" would come along soon after the wedding.

Her mother must have bought those things when

Randi was ten—before her father had died, and wrapped them carefully to keep them from yellowing. A tear threatened to spill from the corner of her eye and Randi blinked it away. There would be no children or happily-ever-afters from this union, but Randi was determined to make the best use of her mother's hopes, anyway.

"I didn't see your stepfather outside. Will you wait for him in case he's late?"

Marian's question dragged her back into the present. "I didn't invite him. I haven't told him about Manny...or the wedding."

"He'll find out, you know. In fact, he probably already knows. It's impossible to keep a secret around this place for long."

"Oh, I don't mind if he finds out after we're married. But I just didn't want him here today. Lewis Lee and Hannah are my family now. They're here and you're here. That's all that matters."

"Randi." Marian's eyes filled with tears and she hugged her friend. "You know I'll always be there for you."

Now Randi felt like crying. How she wished she was really getting married and not telling her dear friend these fibs.

Marian stepped back and smiled at her. "You look perfect." She folded her arms over her chest and grinned past the tears welling up in her eyes. "I have a little surprise wedding present for you, hon."

"Oh, I wish you hadn't done that. I told you not to get us anything."

"This is different. I know you two can't take a full-fledged honeymoon right now, and I figured what with the books that you've been reading and all that... well..."

Randi felt herself flush again and hung her head.

"So I've arranged to give you two a little privacy tonight. Lacy Anderson will take Ricky for the night, and when you and Manny get home you'll find a couple of special care packages I made up for you."

Lacy Anderson was Randi's boss at the school where she worked. Ricky would be perfectly safe and probably very happy staying with her and her family for the night. But Randi wasn't sure how Manny might take the separation from the baby. He was so protective because the baby's life might be in danger. Even Randi felt a bit of panic at the thought of losing sight of Ricky.

"Thank you for the thought, Marian. But can we take a rain check? I think Manny would rather we'd all be together as a family our first night as man and wife."

"All right then...anytime you want a break, just let me know. The offer stands."

"You're so kind." Randi's guilt about the lies grew.

"Well, the care package you'll find in the kitchen pantry is okay for Manny to open with you," Marian began. "But the one I left upstairs in your bedroom might be a little embarrassing for him to see. Maybe you should look at it first and decide if you want to make use of the things it contains tonight or not."

Randi giggled, and the two women hugged again.

Manny's knees felt weak as he stood in the office of the county judge waiting for Randi. Thank God Witt Davidson had arrived this morning to stand up with him. Witt just might be required to physically hold him up before this whole thing was over. Of course, if that happened, Witt would never let him forget it.

Witt, who'd recently retired from the FBI to run a foster ranch in South Texas with his new wife, was the closest thing to a buddy that Manny had ever had. The two worked together a while back as part of an undercover assignment on a ranch located at the border. He'd come today at Reid's request to make Manny's commitment to this wedding appear all the more real.

Most men on their wedding day felt the need to have at least some family or friends in attendance. And, of course, Manny could never have had his real family come to a fake wedding. They would have taken the whole thing in the wrong way. How could he expect them to understand?

Right about now, Manny wasn't too sure himself how to take this phony wedding. It all seemed too real.

"Wow, Sanchez, this is sure some tough assignment you've drawn," Witt whispered as Randi entered the room and took her place beside Manny.

Manny scowled at his altogether too-blond friend. The physical differences between the two men stood out today in a way that irked Manny to no end.

He glared into Witt's blue eyes and snarled through his pursed lips. "Quiet, Davidson, or you're outta here."

Privately, though, Manny had to agree with Witt. In his whole worthless life, he'd never seen anything as stunning as Randi looked today. What a picture she made.

She'd swept her hair up in a loose topknot making the tiny pearl drops dangling from her earlobes easy to spot. Her dress nipped in tightly at her waist and was accentuated by the tiny rose corsage he'd given her. She reminded him of a woman from some earlier time, but she had a modern swing to her step and a new glint in her eyes.

Once more it was those eyes that captured his soul. Clear green, ringed with deepest blue, her eyes seemed to gaze right through him, seeing all his weaknesses and doubts.

This was not the smartest thing he'd ever done. He knew that the whole fake wedding deal was bound to end badly. But there was nothing he could do about it now. He squirmed and ran a finger under his collar. How on earth did some men manage to wear tight collars and ties everyday?

Manny tried to keep his gaze on the judge, who read the marriage vows to both of them, but when Randi began to speak, her voice shook. He glanced down at her and saw a noticeable tremble in her hands.

He felt as if someone had put a stake through his heart. Here he was feeling sorry for himself when she was the one who'd agreed to go along with his cover story, lied to her friends and had totally changed her life for his sake. She was the one who would have to face whatever small-town gossip this fake marriage caused when Operation Rock-a-Bye was only a dim memory.

He reached over and took her hand in his. She jerked slightly when he touched her, then calmed noticeably as he tried to give her his warmth. What else could he do for her? He couldn't do much, and yet he owed her everything.

Somehow they got through the quick ceremony. At the end he placed an imitation gold wedding band on her finger. Another fake. What a perfect statement about his whole life—phony.

Manny knew the drill. A kiss was mandatory. When he turned to face her, he noticed the slight quiver in her chin and the too-bright shine in her eyes. And he was lost.

He'd meant it to be a quick smack on the lips, but when he felt the hard, sensual promise in her tender response, he became tormentingly aware of the softness in her body and the underlying innocence in her scent. As the kiss intensified, he nibbled at her bottom lip and tried to remember why their being married was a bad thing.

"Whoa, buddy." Witt jammed an elbow in Manny's ribs, bringing him back to reality with a thump. "Give the rest of the poor men on earth a last crack at heaven, will you?"

Witt enthusiastically twirled Randi around. "Mind if the best man gets a kiss from the bride?" Though her eyes were wide, she smiled and murmured okay. Witt planted a huge wet smack on her lips as she erupted in giggles. A red haze clouded Manny's eyes as he grabbed his friend's arm and dragged him away from her. After they were separated, Manny took two deep breaths and unfisted his hands.

*It's not real.* This is all an act, he reminded himself.

No one's getting married for real. No one is really in love.

Kisses and hugs all around quickly followed, covering up Manny's embarrassment at overreacting.

A couple of hours later, safely back at the ranch, Randi served their guests glasses of punch. Manny had been wishing for something stronger. Much stronger.

Randi was holding up her end of this charade rather well. She looked for all the world like a blushing bride. Manny wanted to find something else to hold his attention, but, try as he might, his eyes kept coming back to her.

The rest of the small assemblage seemed fairly amicable. Lewis Lee and Witt were having a serious discussion in a corner about the finer points of cattle insemination. Hannah and Marian were fussing over Ricky as if he were the last kid on earth, while Randi flitted back and forth across the huge kitchen passing around little bits of food.

Standing in a corner out of the way, Manny had just taken another sip of punch when the back door burst open and a heavy-set man smashed through the mud room and exploded into the kitchen.

"What the hell is going on here?" the stranger bellowed.

"F-F-Frank. We… I…" Randi took a couple of steps and stood in front of the man, while the rest of the group silently stared at the intruder. Whoever this character was, he'd certainly put a damper on the day.

"Well, daughter, what little bit of treachery are you attempting behind my back?"

*Hell's fire!* Manny set his glass down on the counter. This jerk was her stepfather? No wonder she hadn't invited him to the wedding.

Manny watched as Randi subtly set her shoulders and regained a grasp on her control. He clamped down on his own growing anger, for her sake. She wouldn't want him to make any kind of scene, so he remained where he was. But he grew wary and ready to move if need be.

Ignoring both her stepfather's words and his tone, Randi kept her voice calm. "I'd like to introduce you to my new husband." She turned, her gaze finding Manny's, and reached her hand in his direction. "Manny Sanchez, this is my stepfather Frank Riley. We were married this afternoon, Frank. Won't you join us in a toast?"

Manny wasn't sure, but looking at the man, he didn't think he'd ever seen anybody's face get quite that shade of red before. It was more purple than red, actually.

On pure instinct, Manny took a step toward Randi.

While he mused about the color of the man's face, Frank suddenly flew at Randi and grabbed her by the shoulders. "You must be out of your mind. I'll have it annulled," he yelled.

Manny was moving toward them in earnest now.

Frank shook her with such force he nearly lifted her off her feet. "You stupid, stubborn little witch! After all I've done for you…all I've offered to do. I would've made us both rich. Instead you marry this…this wet-back?"

Frank reared his hand back, and before Manny could reach them, he slapped Randi across the face, sending her reeling backward onto the floor.

The next few seconds were a blur.

From somewhere Manny thought he heard a savage growl, but then that might have come from him. Anything was a possibility because the next time Manny was cognizant, Witt was dragging him off Frank—who was laying on the floor shaking and begging for help through lips that were spouting blood and would most likely swell to twice their normal size.

Lewis Lee hauled Frank off the floor but kept a firm grip on him. Behind Witt's shielding body, Manny knew Marian and Hannah had gone to Randi's aid and that Ricky was still in his playpen, screaming at the top of his lungs. Through the chaos and past the burning desire to put his hands around Frank's chubby neck and squeeze until the man's eyes popped out of his head, Manny heard Randi's faltering voice.

"Please, Manny, don't. Leave him alone. He's not worth it."

# Eight

Manny jerked his fingers back out of the bowl of hot water, nearly tipping his chair over in the process. "Ow. You want to give me blisters, too?"

Witt chuckled and, feigning a serious pout, sat down next to him at the kitchen table. "Poor baby. Did that nasty old water give you an owwie?"

Over an hour ago Lewis Lee and Hannah had pushed Frank out the back door amid threats of legal retribution against everyone in the room. Manny wasn't the slightest bit worried about the threats, but he was concerned about Randi. He hadn't seen her since he'd helped her up off the kitchen floor and Marian had spirited her upstairs.

"Just shut up, Davidson, and stick an ice cube in the bowl, will you?" He glared at his friend, grumbling.

"Wuss." Witt shoved Manny's injured knuckles back down into the warm water laced with liniment. "It's good for you."

"Damn, Witt." Manny felt like an idiot. "What the hell happened to me? I've never lost my cool like that on an assignment before. I'm supposed to be a professional."

"Maybe this assignment is different." Witt leaned back in his chair and scrutinized him. "Maybe you've become, uh, emotionally involved with this one."

Manny spat out a few choice phrases, sinking lower in his chair with each word.

The back door suddenly banged open. That son of a bitch wouldn't have the nerve to show his face back here, would he?

Lewis Lee strode into the kitchen alone. "Thought you might have a couple of sore knuckles." He eased himself into an empty chair at the table facing Manny. "So I brought you something to take the sting out."

He set a bottle of whisky down in the middle of the table and pulled off the cap. "Good old Frank will be a mite sore for a few days, too. It took six stitches to finally shut that mouth of his." Lewis Lee never smiled, but there was a twinkle in his eyes as he took the first slug from the bottle.

Manny used a free hand to raise the bottle to his lips after Lewis Lee handed it off to him. "Thanks, old man."

He took a big swig and felt the burning sensation clear to his toes. *Damn good. Bootleg booze.* Just what he needed tonight. He took a second sip and felt the welcome relaxation moving up through his limbs as he turned the bottle over to Witt.

Witt used his palm to wipe off the rim of the bottle and took a slug. "Jeez," he gasped. "That's...good stuff."

The three of them passed the bottle around in silence while Manny soaked his knuckles.

Lewis Lee broke their reverie. "Hell of a way to start off your wedding night."

Manny didn't want to be reminded that this was his wedding night. Things were getting mighty fogged up in his brain as it was.

He used his fist as a prop for his temple. "Oh, God, Witt. He hit her. That dirty coward actually hit her, and I couldn't get to him fast enough to stop it."

Witt grabbed the bottle and took another swallow. "You did what you could. I don't believe he'll be thinking about a repeat performance anytime soon."

Manny felt a twitch in his eye and set his jaw. "I should have killed him. I *will* kill him if he ever tries to hurt her again."

He wanted to think, but things were getting hazy. Facts seemed to be missing or obscured.

Manny directed a question to Lewis Lee. "Can you tell me what Frank's outburst was all about?"

The older man scratched the day-old whiskers on his chin. "I suppose I can make an educated guess. Frank's been talking about dividing up the Running C ever since he married Randi's mama. He's had it in his head, all this time, that wealthy retirees from San Antonio or Austin would pay a pretty penny to become hobby ranchers. 'Break it up into five-acre plots. There's a fortune to be made for a clever man,' he's always saying."

Lewis Lee took another swallow of the whisky and then looked down into the bottle, as if not sure there would be one more drink left. "Since the missus passed away, I know he's been pestering Randi to sign some papers giving him the right to do what he wants."

"Do each of them own part of the ranch?" Manny probed.

Lewis Lee shrugged. "Ain't none of my business."

Manny struggled to understand. "She doesn't want to divide the ranch?"

"Randi promised her pappy on his deathbed that she'd never let anything happen to the place. She were only ten at the time, but she took her vow to heart. I believe she'd just about starve to death rather than let a bunch of 'come-here,' old geezers squat on Cullen land."

"Is that a real possibility…starving to death?" Manny was beginning to piece a few things together about the woman who was now his wife.

"Naw." Lewis Lee ran a hand over his jaw. "Well… maybe."

Manny heard someone coming down the hall and turned around expectantly.

"Good evening, gentlemen." Marian moved into the kitchen, picked the empty bottle up off the table and pitched it in the trash. "It's time to call an end to this little party."

She folded her arms across her chest and waited.

"Ahem." Lewis Lee cleared his throat and backed his chair away from the table. "I guess I'll be going along home."

Marian stood between Lewis Lee and the mud room door. "You and Hannah can take Witt in for the night, can't you?"

"Wait a second, Marian," Manny began irritably.

"It's okay, son." Lewis Lee waved off Manny's objections. "It's too late to drive him back to town, and I think I see her point. After all, it *is* your wedding night."

Wedding night. The fake marriage. Operation Rock-a-Bye. It all came back to Manny in a sobering rush.

Lewis Lee and Witt bid the other two good-bye, declaring that a long chilly walk home might just do them some good.

After they'd gone, Marian picked up a sleeping Ricky, taking great care not to wake him. "I'll put the baby to bed, then I'm leaving, too. You'd better get yourself together and head upstairs soon. Your wife needs you."

When Marian had left, the quiet of the house was nearly deafening. In the dark and in his stocking feet, Manny climbed the stairs toward the bedrooms carrying the bottle of champagne and two glasses that he'd found in the pantry.

The bottle had been sitting in a puddle of melted ice— a bittersweet and lonely sight. Randi must have had such high hopes for her fake wedding night. He felt a twang of regret that he'd had to use her so badly…that this wasn't a real honeymoon…that he wasn't her real husband.

He owed her at least one drink. Randi had gone to all the trouble to make this marriage appear to be real and, to top it off, she'd had to deal with that bastard of a stepfather. Yeah. Manny figured he owed her a lot more than just one drink.

He knocked on her bedroom door, but got no answer. When he peeked in, he found the bed still made, with Randi's dress carefully laid across it. Ricky was softly snoring in his crib. But where was Randi?

At the end of the darkened hallway, Manny noticed a mellow, reddish glow coming from under his bedroom door. With his curiosity piqued, he pushed open the door and got the shock of a lifetime.

Bathed in that soft red hue, the master bedroom appeared more fantasy than reality. The old heirloom bedspread had been replaced by a red velvet throw, matching exactly the red velvet swags hanging from the windows and bedposts. Some exotic fragrance lay softly in the air, reminding him of the musky smells of summer on the range. It immediately aroused him, and he fought his senses.

As he walked farther into the room, he noted that muted classical music wound its way through the subtle perfume, heating his blood and quickening his breath.

They would have one quick drink and then he'd sleep on the sofa. Randi was too naive. He was too jaded and experienced. This simply was not going to happen.

His eyes quickly adjusted to the light. The vision he beheld of Randi reclining on the bed left him breathless. He'd never seen anyone so beautiful in his entire life. He barely recognized her, but his body began to throb in a way that told him *it* certainly did.

Dressed in a flimsy white nightgown, Randi lay back on a bunch of pillows. Her milky, translucent skin and the nearly see-through gown were in stark contrast to the heavy red velvet. His breath hitched and he almost dropped the bottle.

One side of the gown had risen almost to her hip and afforded him a view of a sheer, white stocking supported by a lacy garter. His blood boiled, racing to parts of him he'd rather not think about right now. He stood speechless, his body screaming at him for release.

"Hi. Is everyone gone?" Her voice was low, sexy but slightly hesitant.

"Uh…" He couldn't think clearly again, but this time it had nothing to do with liquor and everything to do with the woman he'd married earlier that afternoon.

"What're you doing in this bedroom and...uh...what do you think you're going to accomplish with all this?"

Randi fidgeted under his scrutiny. Not totally positive herself what she'd hoped would happen, she couldn't answer him.

"I brought you some of Marian's champagne." He walked over to the bed, set the glasses on the nightstand and poured. He handed her one but was careful not to touch her in any way.

She swallowed the bubbly liquid in one gulp. Whew! Talk about your fizzy bubbles. The stuff tickled her nose, then exploded her insides.

But it gave her a minute to judge his mood. How was he feeling since the scene downstairs? And could she manage to change his mind about them—about her?

"I don't think that's exactly the way champagne is meant to be drunk," he mumbled.

"No? It's good stuff, though, isn't it?" She set the glass back on the nightstand.

Manny nodded and sipped from his own glass, still watching her carefully over the rim.

"I've been studying up on how to please a man. Marian helped me with the room, even though she said tonight might not be the best time for us to get together. What do you think?"

He set his glass down next to hers and inched closer to the bed. "Sweet Randi, we've talked about this before. I'm on a mission. The marriage isn't for real, it's just an assignment."

She grimaced at the thought of how embarrassed she was going to be if she couldn't make him to see her as more than just a job in this getup. All womankind might disown her.

Manny must have misunderstood. He eased himself down on the bed next to her.

*"Dios mio,"* he whispered. "Your beautiful face..." He caressed her cheek with tender touches and gazed at her with such gentleness that she nearly cried.

Randi had forgotten all about the smack across the face Frank had given her. She probably made a dreadful sight. Dang. Well, so much for being sexy and desirable.

Sure enough, Manny jumped away from her and the bed. "I'll get something for your face. Hold on."

Whatever had possessed her to even consider trying to seduce a man like Manny? She must have totally lost her mind. Before she could gather her wits and run back to her own room for a terry cloth robe, he was back sitting beside her on the bed.

"I thought I saw what you needed in the freezer this afternoon," he murmured, placing one of the frozen steaks Marian had provided for their wedding-night dinner against her cheek.

"Oww."

"Easy, sugar. This will help the swelling."

His voice was so kind, so full of concern that she closed her eyes and decided to lie still for whatever he wanted to do. When the stinging stopped, she opened them again and found him searching her face with his gaze.

"It looks painful. Does it hurt very much?"

She didn't...couldn't say anything. No one had ever looked at her with such deep concern before.

"I'm so sorry I got you into this, Randi. It's all my fault."

The light was definitely low, in a pinkish-haze kind of way, but she could swear the man had tears in his eyes. For her pain? He was apparently in more pain over it than she was.

The whole idea got to her in a way she never would have guessed. It turned her on. Now she wanted him more than ever. Now she had to be with him. Be a part of him.

"What can I do to make it up to you?" he murmured.

His words, so close to what she'd been thinking, made her jump.

"Damn. Am I hurting you more?" he asked warily.

"No. No. I just— It's just that I need—" She turned her head in frustration. How would she ever put her desires into words? She had to begin taking control of her own destiny. She'd been passive for long enough. After all, this was probably all she would ever have of life, and she was positively desperate to make the most of it.

Manny set the steak aside and put a gentle finger under her chin, turning her head back to face him. "What, sweetheart? What do you need? What can I do?"

It was now or never for Randi.

With every fiber of her being she made the decision to learn how to get what she wanted—even if it killed her doing it. "Make love with me, Manny. I want desperately to know what it feels like to be with a man."

He dropped his hand and stood. "But you don't want me."

"Yes, I do." How could he not see how much she wanted him?

"But I've never been anyone's 'first' before."

She blurted out what came to her mind. "You wouldn't hurt me."

"I wouldn't know…" He hesitated, searching her face again.

"I trust you more than anyone else to make it right."

He jerked his gaze away and had such a serious look in his eyes that she was certain he was going to refuse her.

Randi was simply devastated. She'd lost.

But a small part of her wouldn't give up—at least not yet. "Manny, please?"

He sighed and turned back to her. "You're really something, you know that?" He set his jaw, then smiled.

She moved across the bed to make room for him, but he continued to stand. She went over in her mind everything she'd learned from the books. "Tell me what will turn you on? What else I can do to get the mood right?"

He chuckled softly, but his eyes held hers with a passion she'd only dreamed about before. "Oh, you've already got it right, sugar. You don't need to do a thing. I've been 'in the mood' since I stepped through the door."

She let her gaze drift downward to his jeans fly and quickly saw the evidence of what he told her. She gulped back a sudden burst of fear. This was no time to be a sissy. All her fantasies were about to come true.

He stood towering over her and lifted a hand to her cheek. "I've wanted you since the first time I saw you. I can't seem to deny you anything, even though I know it's wrong."

"Really? Then…should I undress for you or should you undress me yourself?"

He sat down next to her on the bed and moved his hand to the nape of her neck. "No, honey. We're going to take this slow…easy."

"But I thought you said you wanted me. In the books it says it's hard for a man to wait. It could be bad for you."

This time, the smile lit up his whole face and the mirth in his eyes was obvious.

"Outside of the books, you'll find things between a man and a woman are a lot different than what you've read. I appreciate that you're concerned about my welfare, but let me lead this dance."

"But...the book..."

"Sweet Randi. I want you so badly right now I could rip your clothes off and dive right in." He began to massage her neck. "But that wouldn't make it right for you. It wouldn't be anywhere close to your dreams."

His lips found hers with a softness that destroyed her resolve to do things by the book. The whole world was upside down. The oriental fragrance from the incense she'd set out must be doing something to her brain. As he deepened the kiss, she suddenly felt feverish and fought for each breath.

She didn't realize that his free hand had begun to slide the material of the negligee across her body until the friction caused an ache in her swollen breast and shot an electric current directly to her womb. He eased back slightly from their kiss, and she opened her eyes. His face was shadowed, but she could see that his breathing was also labored, his chest rapidly rising and falling.

"If something gets to be too much for you, you can stop me anytime," he said in a husky voice.

Stop him? All she wanted was for him to speed things up, to ease the tension that was building deep inside her.

Slowly, deliberately he freed her breast from the opaque material. Randi immediately felt the cold air hit her and noticed her breast puckering as a result. How embarrassing.

She tried to squirm away from his gaze, but he held her shoulders and pinned her in place.

"You are so beautiful." He groaned and his gaze followed the flush she knew was beginning to color her body. "I've dreamed about you for days now, but you're even better than my best fantasy."

Her mouth began to water with what she could only imagine was deep desire. A few agonizing moments passed until she could no longer contain herself.

"Aren't you going to touch me?"

"Oh, sugar. I'm still caught up in looking at you. Patience, my sweet." Despite his words he used a finger to trace the outline of her nipple. Gently he stroked, back and forth, making it tighten even more.

He was looking at her breast with a kind of reverence that made her feel adored. But adoration wasn't what she wanted. She wasn't entirely sure what she wanted, but it was more—much more. Then he cupped her breast so carefully it made her arch her back, pressing herself against his palm.

"Ah, Randi." Taking a shaky breath, he dipped his head and took her aching nipple into his mouth.

*Oh, my.* That was what she'd been waiting for.

The swirl of his tongue, the warmth of his hot, moist mouth and the sweet pressure as he sucked, made her feel a corresponding heat between her legs. She arched her back even higher, trying to stem the aches she felt running from her breasts to the juncture of her thighs. He moved to her other breast and lavished it with the same attention, while continuing to massage the damp nipple he'd just left.

She found herself twisting and moaning with the exquisite pressure. "Please. Please."

"Do you want me to stop?"

"No. I want...I want..."

She felt his warm palm slide up the inside of her thigh and shook all over at his touch.

"Is this what you want, sweetheart?"

His hand moved between her thighs and pressed against the damp silk of her panties. *Oh, yes. Oh, yes.* She wanted to tell him, but he'd lifted his head and kissed his way up her neck and across her chin back to her mouth.

For a second she wondered where the wetness on her panties had come from, but soon she couldn't think clearly enough to wonder about anything. It was all she could do not to beg him to hurry up.

As if he sensed her impatience, he raised his head and leaned his forehead against hers. "Slow and easy is going to win this race, sweet Randi. I'm right here with you. Hold on to me and go with your feelings. Don't think."

He tenderly kissed her forehead and placed tiny kisses on her nose, cheeks and finally her lips. Somewhere in the middle of all that, his hand had moved to the waistband of her panties. He ran his fingers along the outline of the waistband in a bewitching motion. When he slipped his hand beneath the silk and lightly slid his fingers down through her intimate curls, she jerked.

His hand stilled. "Is that a no?"

"No," she gasped. "I mean… I was just surprised at the feelings. Please, don't stop."

"Yes, ma'am. Your wish is my…" The smile in his voice warmed her more than the kiss he placed on her lips.

She began to quiver and tried hard to remember his words. Her first impulse was to tighten her thighs and fist her hands with tension. But he'd told her to relax. If he was the one she trusted not to hurt her, then she was determined to follow his instructions. Besides, the feelings in her body were too delicious to miss. She wanted to experience it all.

She grabbed at his shoulders and hung on for dear life.

He pulled his hand away, used it to lift her hips and used the other hand to pull at her panties, sliding them down and off in one smooth movement. Her breathing became more difficult. She felt as if someone had turned her into a liquid mass of steaming jelly.

Manny moaned. ''Ah, hell. You are the most perfect, the most beautiful woman.''

He moved a tentative finger to the sensitive nub at the very heart of her. As he lightly touched there, shivers moved down her spine and this time when she arched, it was her buttocks that raised toward the pleasure he provided.

Randi felt him separate her legs and situate himself between them. He leaned over to kiss her breasts once more.

This must be it, she thought. In a second he'll remove his own clothes and it will be over. Finally she'd taken an active part in deciding her own fate. She was about to become a real woman and the most generous-spirited man on earth was right here to help her through.

Randi tried hard not to tense up in preparation.

# Nine

"**Y**ou're thinking again," Manny whispered against Randi's skin.

"Oh, sorry," she mumbled in a husky voice.

He knew she was close. But it had to be exactly right.

"Stay with me, Randi. Just breathe and feel the sensations running through you. Your body will do the rest."

He began kissing his way down her glorious body heading for the target he'd been longing to taste. When he reached her belly button, he ringed it with his tongue and she moaned deep in her throat. He had to grit his teeth, holding back his own growing needs.

With gentle strokes of his tongue, he worked lower, nipping and sucking lightly as he went. His mouth found the soft fuzz covering her mound. When he playfully tugged some of the hair with his teeth, Randi gasped and bucked her hips.

Yeah, now she was getting into it.

He was getting into it, as well. Her satiny skin smelled and tasted like paradise. Subtle and tantalizing.

He moved lower still and let his tongue find the object of his desire. He licked her once…twice and then blew a cooling breath across her nub.

Putting a finger deep inside her and withdrawing once again to flick his tongue over her was maddening agony for him. But it was having the desired effect on Randi.

"Come on, baby," he urged. "Let go. You taste so good. I want it all."

She screamed as the convulsions pulsed through her. Manny grabbed her up, wrapped his arms around her in a bear hug and held on tight. He felt the quivers of release sweep her into a land of fantasies. He couldn't help but cover her face with tiny, triumphant kisses.

When her breathing evened out, she giggled into his kisses. Ah, what a feeling, he thought. For once in his life he'd actually done something special for someone. He'd brought a sweet and kind woman to her first climax—and better yet, he'd made her laugh like a schoolgirl.

"So… Was it as good as the books say?" He smiled against her shoulder, then placed another quick kiss on her glistening skin.

"Oh, yes. It was…it was…better than anything I'd ever dreamed." Her voice was sweet and lazy, and still slightly out of breath. "But you haven't…and I'm still… It can't be over yet."

Manny almost giggled himself at her innocent question.

"It's over for now, sugar. I don't have any protection for us. I wasn't expecting to need anything like that tonight."

"But you said you'd be the one."

"Yeah, and I intend to keep my promise. We'll take one step at a time. Ease into it, so to speak. Tonight was just the first step."

"Oh, no. You mean I have to wait? How long?"

"Sounds as if you might have liked what we did here enough to want more. Is that right?" He couldn't resist teasing her, and filling his pride while he was at it.

"I loved it! You must know I did." She blushed a beautiful shade that matched the glow in the room perfectly. "But when can we…finish the deed?"

The truth was that if she didn't stop moving under him, he might just "finish the deed" alone—and soon.

She turned her head, trying to find his eyes. "Wait a minute. How about you? Is it supposed to be your turn now?"

He felt her fingers at his fly and almost bit his tongue. "Whatcha doing there, girl?" he asked as casually as he could manage.

She was young and inexperienced. She couldn't be expected to understand a man's body or how to satisfy him without the need for birth control.

"If you'd roll off me a bit, I could reach things better." She fumbled with the buttons of his jeans. "How do these buttons work, anyway? They seem all backward."

"Look, honey. You don't have to do anything for me. Just give me a few minutes and I'll be fine. Tomorrow night we'll take care of…"

"There!" She'd managed to undo his fly and had run into the cotton briefs he'd forgotten he had on.

She began rubbing him through the cotton, and his erection stiffened even more at her touch. As if he'd needed any help.

"I've been reading up about some techniques I'd like to try," she whispered. "Is it okay with you?"

This just might be the most erotic thing that had ever happened to him. Never in his life had a woman approached him like this. And that it was Randi, a complete beginner, to boot—well, that was almost too much to take.

In fact, it was definitely too much for him to take. He clamped his fingers around her wrist and pulled her hand away from his groin.

"That's enough for tonight, sweetheart. We can learn more about each other tomorrow night." He leaned over and placed a kiss on the tender juncture of her neck and shoulder.

"But what about you? This doesn't seem fair."

He couldn't help but grin against her shoulder. "Wait a minute here. Just which one of us has had experience in this area?"

She giggled at him and he tickled her rib cage.

"Hey! Stop that!" she managed through her laughter.

"All right! *You* have," she yelped with delight. "You're the one who knows what he's doing."

"There you go, then. I'm the teacher and you're the student. Let me decide how this is going to go down."

He pinned her arms to her sides in another bear hug and rolled them both over, keeping her close to his chest. On her side, Randi pulled her knees toward her chest and allowed Manny to spoon himself behind her.

Being cozy, warm and easy with a woman were a few more of the things he'd not experienced in a very long time, if ever. For one ridiculous moment a glimpse of another kind of life—a better and more joyful life than he'd ever known—stopped him cold. He'd been alone for so long, connecting to no one, taking comfort from no one.

Just when he began to daydream about leading a different life with Randi, he heard her breath hitch and was positive he felt her try to muffle a sob.

"What's the matter, honey? Are you okay?" he whispered in her ear.

"I'm so sorry," she moaned half into the pillow.

"Sorry? For what? Not…"

He didn't want her to regret what they'd done together—or what they were yet to do. No recriminations, no regrets, no ties. That was the way their relationship had to be.

"Oh, no. Not for *that*." She tried to turn in his arms, but he held her tight. He figured she might be better able to talk to him if she didn't have to face him.

"Everything was really wonderful for me, Manny. I'm just sorry I wasn't better prepared. I should have thought of the protection. I know you're miserable and it's all my fault. I should be more experienced. I should have read up some more on what to do. I should have—"

"Shush, honey. Everything's fine. I'm not miserable."

Randi could feel his hot breath on the back of her neck and the press of his erection through his jeans against her bottom. Well, if he wasn't miserable, she'd be miserable enough for both of them.

"Please talk to me." *Oh, for heaven's sake.* Her voice sounded so needy. She didn't want him to think of her that way. "If you're not miserable, what're you feeling?"

He hesitated a second, and she wished she could see his expression.

"I guess the thing I feel the most is gratitude."

"Huh? For what?"

"I'm grateful that you'd trust me enough to want me to be the first." The deep pitch of his husky voice caused her exposed nerve endings to quiver.

He sighed deeply and continued. "Watching you come apart in my arms for the first time in your life was one of the most gratifying experiences in *my* whole worthless life." He shifted slightly behind her but never loosened his grip. "It's a great gift you've bestowed on me, Randi Cullen."

*Oh, dang.* That was one of the sweetest things she'd ever heard. She'd been having enough trouble controlling the tears before. Now what was she going to do?

She swallowed hard and fought for a steady voice. "Can we...can you...talk to me for a while? Tell me about your life. Have you ever been married?"

He laughed lightly into her hair. "No. I've never been lucky enough to meet a woman who could put up with my lifestyle. I joined the bureau right out of college. I've been doing undercover work for Operation Rock-a-Bye ever since."

His voice was filled with slumberous amusement. "I'm out in the field most of the time, sugar. I don't even have a real home. I live out of suitcases and backpacks. It's not the kind of life you'd ask a woman to share."

"But...you're not going to be doing that kind of thing all your life, are you? I mean, don't you want to put down roots someday?"

She could feel his breath steadying, becoming more and more even and controlled.

"I doubt it. You see, I wasn't raised that way. My

parents came across the river from Mexico before I was born.''

"Oh, dear heavens." She nearly wept. "No wonder you flew at Frank when he called you that name. I'm so sorry."

"Don't be. I've been called much worse. The only reason I attacked your stepfather was because he hit you. Has he ever done that before?"

"No. Never. And it doesn't matter. Tell me more about your parents." She could scarcely believe that a man had fought for her sake, and she didn't want to think of the implications of that right now.

"Before I could even walk, they became migrant farm workers, traveling with the seasons and the changing crops."

"Migrant farm workers…really? How did you ever manage to get to college?"

His silence shouted at her in a tone louder than she could bear. Whatever had possessed her to ask such a thing?

"I'm sorry again," she added quickly. "I didn't mean that migrants weren't smart enough for college. I just meant how did you find the time to go to high school, the dedication to stick it out, the money?"

"Don't be sorry. Those aren't such outrageous questions. I have six brothers and sisters, and none of them ever considered going to college. In fact, only a couple of them managed to graduate from high school."

He eased away from her and flipped onto his back. Randi turned and was glad she could at least now see his profile. It would be simpler to listen to him if she could judge his facial expressions.

"Then how'd you do it?"

"Pure stubbornness, I suppose."

She expected a grin with that pronouncement, but his expression never changed.

"No, really," he continued. "What I had was a fairy godfather. One year, when I had just turned fourteen, my family was in the Rio Grande Valley for the fall grapefruit crop. My parents were forced to enroll us all in school, even though they intended to take us out to help with the picking when the time came.

"One of my teachers was an ex-cop. Apparently, he saw something in me that no one else had. He took an interest in a poor kid who could barely speak English and who didn't own a decent pair of shoes. He tutored me. He badgered me into studying. And when picking time rolled around, he pleaded with my father to let me come live with his family and continue in school."

"What a great thing to do. Did he pay for your schooling, too?"

Even in the dim light, she could see him shake his head.

"I earned a scholastic scholarship to a small college in North Texas, and what that didn't pay for I earned with a part-time job in the cafeteria. I guess he was basically right about me."

"So, you went into FBI work to honor him?" Randi asked quietly.

"Naw." He chuckled lightly. "I did it to spite him. He tried his damnedest to get me interested in some safer, saner occupation. I think he had his heart set on me being a college professor or something."

It was Randi's turn to chuckle at the image of this big, dangerous man lecturing to a roomful of students.

"Do you get a chance to visit with him much these days?"

"He died a few years back," he said sadly. "I do

keep in touch with his widow, though. I still feel like their house is the only home I've ever known."

She wasn't quite sure what to say to him. His upbringing was so different from hers. She laid her head on his shoulder and let the conversation lag. The peace she suddenly felt wound a quiet contentment through her. She closed her eyes for just a second.

Randi must have dropped off to sleep because the next thing she knew, a noise and violent shaking awoke her with a start. It took her a second to remember where she was. Her first panicked thoughts were that Ricky must need attention, but when she oriented herself she realized that the noises were close by—in the same bed with her.

Manny was moaning and groaning, flailing his arms and kicking out with his legs. "No. No. Stop that!" he thundered. "I can't…I can't reach you. I'm coming!"

For a second Randi was frightened. But upon closer inspection, she realized that his eyes were closed and many of his screams were really garbled words. Manny was having a nightmare.

Without thinking, she reached for him. When she touched his clammy skin, he sat bolt upright and grabbed for her.

"Manny, stop. Hey! Oww," she cried as he squeezed her arm.

He tightened his grip on her shoulders.

"Manny, please. You're hurting me."

The pleading tone in her voice apparently did the trick. His eyes opened wide with shock.

"Ah, *Dios mio!* Randi, honey, did I hurt you?" He pulled her to his chest and wrapped his arms around her.

Randi felt the tremors rocking through his body as he held her close. "I'm okay. You were having a nightmare."

"I...I guess I was." He breathed into her hair.

"What was it about? Was someone hurting you?"

"No. It wasn't me that was being hurt. It was..."

Manny released her and rolled out of bed. He was still fully dressed, except for his boots. He headed toward the other bedroom in a kind of daze, absently buttoning his fly as he went.

"Where are you going?" Randi's voice penetrated his haze, but he couldn't answer—couldn't talk or breathe—until he made sure.

In a few broad steps, he entered the stillness of the other bedroom and went straight to the baby's crib. Ricky lay there on his back. Some of the glow from the master bedroom seeped into the room through the black night, giving Manny a good chance to see the boy's chest as he quietly breathed in and out in his sleep.

Ricky was alive and well. Manny took his first breath since getting up.

"What's the matter? Is something wrong with Ricky?" Randi whispered softly.

She appeared beside Manny and gazed down at the child sleeping peacefully in his crib. "Oh. Was it Ricky you were trying to save in your dream?"

"I don't know." That was as honest an answer as he could come up with right now.

He shook his head, trying to clear away the wispy strands of sleep. The baby was okay. Randi was okay. And he...

He turned his hands over and studied his palms in the dim light. They shook violently, and the sweat was clearly visible.

"That must have been some nightmare," Randi said wearily.

He'd had a few similar nightmares in his life, but none

were this bad. He could still feel the fear and the urgent need to do something. The problem was, he never could see who he was trying to save—didn't know who it was that needed his help so desperately.

He'd thought it must have been Ricky. But looking down on the baby now, he just couldn't place the boy in his nightmare. In fact, the whole thing was receding into the blackness of his subconscious.

Frustrating.

"Go back to bed, Randi. I'm going to work."

"Work? It's three in the morning."

He turned and walked out into the hall. "Go back to bed," he called over his shoulder.

Still wet and shivering from his cold shower, Manny headed down the stairs toward the mud room for his work boots. He'd thought a good cold shower would work out the irritations of his frustrating night with Randi and then his confusing and terrifying dream. But the shower hadn't helped. It was just cold.

Now he was frustrated, confused, terrified—and freezing as well.

When he entered the kitchen, it suddenly occurred to him why his stomach had been grumbling since he'd started down the stairs. Randi was making breakfast. And she had the coffee ready.

"What are you doing?" he growled at her. "I thought I told you to get some more sleep."

"My. Aren't we crabby this morning." Randi poured a mug of coffee and shoved it at him as he passed behind her.

"Look, Randi." He stopped and automatically took a sip of the coffee in his hand. "You do not have to get up and fix me breakfast. You're not really my wife. I don't expect you to act that way. I don't want you to act that way.''

''Hmm. You want your eggs scrambled or sunny side up?'' She turned back to the stove at about the same time as the toast popped from the toaster.

''I don't want any eggs.'' He set the coffee down on the counter and, putting his hands on his hips stared at her back.

She went right on cooking without saying a word.

''Randi, stop it. I don't eat breakfast. The coffee is enough.''

She finally turned around. ''You need more than coffee. You should have something more substantial in your stomach.'' Grabbing a plate, she dished up the scrambled eggs and, adding a couple pieces of toast, she set it on the table.

''Now sit and eat.'' She pulled out his chair and then sat down beside it. ''And while you're eating, maybe you can tell me about that dream you had that upset you so much.''

''Damn it, woman! I am not eating breakfast, and I'm not going to talk about any stupid dream,'' he argued. ''Your ranch is falling down around your ears, for cripe's sake. I'm going to finish replacing the fence Lewis Lee and I started the other day. Then I'm going into town to try to find someone who might have some knowledge that'll help me locate the bad guy for Operation Rock-a-Bye.'' He strode into the mud room and picked up a boot.

She got up from the table and moved toward him. ''You're going to town?'' Her eyes sparkled as she beamed at him with a playful little grin. ''Then do you want to go to the store or should I?''

He struggled to put the boot on his foot. As he

stomped down on the heel, he tried to figure out what her smile had been all about. This was sure one confusing woman.

"I don't know if I'll have a chance to stop at a store. What do you need?" he asked.

"Uh...I guess I can take care of it," she said in a surprisingly depressed tone.

The other boot went on smoothly, and he grabbed his coat. "Okay, great. Don't plan on me for supper. I haven't any idea how long I'll be gone." He shoved his arms into the coat sleeves and opened the door.

"Manny," Randi called out to him. "You won't forget your promise, will you?"

*Promise? What promise?* Suddenly, he remembered. *Damn.*

As he stepped into the dark morning, he found he couldn't even look her in the eyes. "Better get some rest today, Randi. I could be real late."

# Ten

Randi was tired and irritable for most of that day. Even Ricky fussed and whined through the morning as though he shared her troubles. When he refused to go down for his after-lunch nap, she was near her wits end.

To top off the simply wonderful day, Hannah stopped in with one of her casseroles, wanting to pry about Manny's background and proceeding to give loads of unwanted advice about how to calm the baby. Randi nearly wept with frustration.

Finally, when she was sure she couldn't take another minute of Ricky's cries and Hannah's nosy questions, Marian's car pulled into the yard. Her friend sized up the situation in a few seconds and swept Hannah out with a few well-chosen words.

As the sound of Hannah's truck receded into the late-afternoon wind, Marian turned her attention to Ricky and Randi. "So. You two look like you've both had a bad night. Didn't things go the way you planned with Manny? Or did the baby end up coming between you?''

Randi picked Ricky up from his playpen and began patting his back as she walked him around the kitchen. ''Ricky was a perfect angel last night. Slept right through. I don't know what's wrong with him now. Maybe he's coming down with something.''

''You didn't answer my question, hon.'' Marian had to raise her voice to be heard over the baby's sobs. ''Did the change of room and the champagne get the desired results from your new husband?''

It was all too much for Randi. Nothing seemed right.

''Oh, Marian. It almost worked. I thought it had, but then he stopped without finishing. He said he didn't have protection and we'd have to do it another time.''

The minute the words were out of her mouth, Randi couldn't believe she'd actually said them. She must really be frustrated and tired to admit such a thing, even to a best friend. The day was steadily going from bad to much worse.

Marian narrowed her eyes at Randi. ''And you couldn't sleep after that?''

''Manny had a nightmare and left for work at 3:00 a.m. I couldn't go back to sleep from worrying about him.''

''Uh-huh. And frustration had nothing to do with it, I'm sure.'' Marian dragged the baby from Randi's arms and jiggled him up and down. ''I have an idea. Why don't I go into town and pick up what you need from the drugstore. I'll take Ricky with me. Maybe the ride will lull him to sleep, and you can get in a nap while we're gone.''

Randi could feel herself flush with embarrassing skin prickles. Served her right for being so open. The trouble

was, she wanted that nap and a few minutes of quiet
more than she cared about her pride. She also wanted to
make sure Manny had no more excuses tonight.

"You wouldn't mind? It would be such a blessing if
you could."

"Sweetie, I told you I'd always try to be there for
you, and I meant it...even if it means buying condoms
from someone who's bound to spread rumors." She hesitated only a moment. "As a matter of fact, it might be
fun to give the town something new to gossip about."

Manny put one foot in front of the other as he dragged
himself up the stairs to Randi's back porch. The purple
twilight had just given way to the soothing darkness of
night. The day had turned out to be even more frustrating
than last night. He bent to pull off his mud-caked boots
and felt every aching second of his thirty-four years.

From the minute he'd reached the missing row of
fence posts he and Lewis Lee had dug and placed a few
days ago, Manny's irritations steadily multiplied. Someone had stolen the posts right out of the ground, then
they'd cut up the bulk of the barbed wire he'd set aside
to use.

He'd had no choice but to borrow Lewis Lee's truck
and head to town at daylight, taking Witt along with him
to talk to the sheriff about the vandalism.

After he'd loaded new supplies at the hardware store,
Manny told the clerk to put it on the Running C's tab
and was promptly asked for cash. "That girl ain't had a
tab in over six months. She's already into the store for
more'n the ranch'll earn in a year," the clerk said.

"How'd she ever get in such bad shape?" Manny
asked.

"Well, I reckon if it weren't for bad luck she'd have

no luck at all. Seemed like she'd just get over one catastrophe when the next one came round.'' The clerk shrugged his shoulders. "Funny, though, I'd have figured she'd be smart enough to keep her head above water or to sell out with a good offer. She ain't done neither. And I know her stepfather has had a decent buyer on the line for months now.''

At the mention of Frank Riley, Manny decided to seek a few answers. "Randi's stepfather has quite a temper, doesn't he?''

The clerk slanted him a curious glance but answered him. "Naw. Not really. Ain't never heard of him blowing up with nobody...'cepting the help occasionally. But then he's had to be traveling a lot over the past years. I guess he could've changed some in that time.''

After Manny paid the man, he'd met up for a few minutes with Witt and Reid, who told him the sheriff had said basically the same thing about Randi and her ranch. Manny didn't understand it. He'd known her long enough now to be sure she was bright, and the past couple of days he'd even noticed a strength of spirit he'd completely missed in her at first. So what was really going on?

Manny didn't believe in bad luck. He was positive that people made their own luck. Was it possible that Randi was deliberately sabotaging herself in order to get away from the ranch?

"You're not as late as I'd thought you might be.'' The sound of Randi's soft voice greeted him as he entered the warmth of her fragrant kitchen.

When he spotted her, holding Ricky with one arm and checking on something in the oven with the other, all thoughts of Operation Rock-a-Bye and the ranch quickly disappeared. She'd put her hair back in that wispy braid

again, and an old-fashioned, checked apron covered her
T-shirt and jeans to the knees. She looked so much as
though she belonged right here, taking care of a baby
and waiting for him to come through the door, that he
had to shake himself to get his mind back on reality.

"It wasn't a very fruitful day. I didn't get much ac-
complished, I'm afraid."

"Did you finish the fence line?"

He didn't want to be the one to tell her about more
trouble on the ranch. He had a feeling it might just be
too much for her to take right now. "Yeah, but it took
longer than I'd figured."

She closed the oven door and put Ricky down in his
playpen.

"Randi."

She swiveled, turning those ever-changing and mirac-
ulous green eyes on him and giving him her full attention. Suddenly he felt as if he might be the only worthwhile man on earth. But still, he wasn't good enough for
her—not by a long shot.

"What would you like to do if you couldn't live on
the ranch anymore?" he prompted.

She laughed. "Yeah, I know things on the ranch are
that bad. I've just been hanging on by see-through tape
for months now."

Sighing deeply, she began to set the supper table
while she kept on talking. "If I had the money, I'd quit
work in the nursery and go to college full time to become a certified teacher. That's been my dream. But it's
way out of the realm of possibility, so I haven't given
it much thought lately."

"Was the amount your stepfather offered for the land
enough to get your dream?"

"I suppose." Her voice was suddenly stilted and she

sounded a bit irritated. "I never took the offer seriously enough to check."

When she looked up from the table, he could see the pain in her heart, clouding over those stunning eyes. He couldn't bear to see her look that way.

"So...how was your day?" he asked. "You look terrific. Did you enjoy the peace and quiet of having me gone all day?"

She chuckled at him, and the sadness in her face gave way to mirth. The look suited her, making him think of home and chocolate chip cookies for some reason.

"Up until the last couple of hours, it wasn't terribly peaceful here. Hannah dropped off her veggie casserole, and if Marian hadn't come by and helped to get rid of her, she'd probably still be here asking questions."

"What did Marian want?"

"You know...I'm not positive. But she offered to take Ricky for a ride while she ran an errand for me. It was a good thing, too. I'd just about had it with him today." She grinned down at the baby, who was contentedly chewing on his knuckles.

"He was being bad?"

"No. But he cried all day."

Manny took a step toward the playpen, but stopped before he reached it. He turned to gaze at her with those strong, quiet eyes.

She was so taken with the look he gave her that she could barely think.

"He doesn't seem the least bit unhappy now," he said.

"The pharmacist told Marian that he's teething. Gave her some gel to put on his gums. I think that must have taken his pain away."

Manny cocked his head and looked confused. "She

took the baby to the drugstore to ask the pharmacist what was wrong with him? Why not a doctor?''

Randi shook her head. ''She went to buy…something else. But she took Ricky in the car to calm him down.''

He started to turn back to the playpen, and Randi thought she'd probably dodged that bullet for a little while longer.

No such luck.

Manny stopped in midstride and swung back around to face her. ''I'm half-afraid to ask. What did you need at the drugstore?''

''You know what…. Did you remember to buy any? I can always take these back if necessary.''

''Damn it, Randi. You asked Marian to buy condoms for us? What were you thinking?''

''I was thinking you might not remember and I was too tired to go to town. You did forget, didn't you?''

Manny shoved his hands on his hips and glared at her. ''Oh, for the love of heaven. What am I going to do with you?''

It wasn't a real curse. In fact, Randi could hear the suppressed laughter in his voice. She decided he must not really be mad, and teasing him could only help the situation.

''You're going to keep your promise, of course. And soon, too. The minute you've eaten and I've fed Ricky, we're going upstairs to make me a real woman.''

She could see him biting his lip to stop the grin she knew he was hiding behind that mask of disapproval. Glad for the lighthearted moment, she figured it might take his mind off how desperate she was acting—and felt.

In the middle of his very tense supper, Manny decided there was too much pressure on both of them. He intended to keep his promise, as much for himself as for Randi, but perhaps forcing it tonight might be unwise.

The trouble was, how to explain that to Randi. Maybe if he volunteered to do some of her chores for her he could soften the blow.

"Let me feed Ricky and put him to bed while you go on upstairs and take a bath. Be lazy. Enjoy yourself. We'll make this the 'be kind to Randi' night."

He could see the indecision in her eyes as she hesitated for a moment. "Well…if you're sure you don't mind. I'd really love a nice hot shower."

The only shower in the house was in the bath off the mud room. Right next to the kitchen. Not what he'd had in mind at all. He'd rather she'd be upstairs so he could give her lots of time. So much time, in fact, that she might fall asleep waiting for him. Now he'd have to think of something else.

"Go on. The baby and I will be fine. I could stand a little time with him, anyway," he murmured.

Randi grinned at him and disappeared upstairs to change.

He picked Ricky up. The wide-eyed baby patted his face and began babbling in that very serious way some babies have.

"Yeah, whatever you say, kid. Let's see if we can't spend a long, long time together tonight."

Manny needn't have worried. It took forever to feed Ricky. For every spoonful of food the baby actually ate, he spit out three more.

Of course, part of the problem might have been that during the feeding Manny's attention was elsewhere. In the shower stall next to the kitchen to be exact.

The sound of the running water in the shower had

shouted to him over the baby's gurgles and squeals. He could picture the water sluicing down over Randi's petal-soft body, going places he'd been last night and desperately wanted to go again.

He pursed his lips and tried to block the erotic images assailing him. Ricky yelped in frustration and Manny realized the hand holding the baby's spoon hung suspended a few inches away from its target.

"Jeez, kid, I'll do better. Hang in there."

With a supreme effort Manny got through the feeding and traipsed upstairs with the baby before Randi came out of the shower. As fumble-fingered as he was in changing Ricky's diaper and putting him into his pj's, Manny was certain that enough time had elapsed to give Randi a chance to fall asleep on his bed waiting for him. At least, he hoped it had. He stood rocking Ricky for an extra half hour just to be sure.

When he finally peered into the master bedroom, he was surprised to find it empty. No red glow. No velvet bed covering. No Randi.

He should have gone to bed right then himself. Wherever she was, she had to be asleep by now. But his curiosity got the better of him.

Manny took a quick tour of the attic, just to be sure that there were no problems with the house she might be trying to solve alone. But she wasn't there, either.

He supposed she had to be downstairs, unless she'd gone outside. It was too cold tonight for any under-the-stars snuggling, although the thought did have a certain appeal.

As he came down the front stairs, he quickly figured out where she had gone. A fire crackled in the front room and the odor of burning mesquite permeated the air with a pungent smell reminiscent of his years in the field. The whole cozy scene was more than compelling.

"Did you have trouble getting Ricky to sleep? Is he okay?" Her voice sounded husky and tenuous, but he couldn't see her through the shadowy light the fire was throwing over the room. He was pretty sure her voice had come from the sofa.

"The baby's fine. Why are you down here instead of upstairs in bed?"

"I tried to wait for you in that big bed, but I got a little...nervous."

She sounded downright scared. He'd known all the pressure would be a mistake. This was no way to have your very first experience of being with a man.

"Randi, honey." He walked to the sofa, bent on one knee before her and kept his voice even. "Why don't we take a rain check on this tonight? Another night when we're both less tired might be better."

Her face was visible in the golden glow of the fire, but he couldn't be sure of her expression. He needed to know how she was feeling—what she was feeling. He simply refused to do or say anything that might hurt her. She was too special, too tender.

"Oh, no, you don't. You promised." She tugged on his shirtsleeve and pulled him up on the sofa with her.

He immediately noticed that she had on her thick terry robe, opened at the collar and belted at the waist. His mind wandered to what she might have on underneath that robe.

"Please, Randi. We need to take things slow." He'd meant every word of that, yet his hand moved to her face.

So smooth, so fine. As he absently rubbed his thumb

over her cheek, he thought of highly polished wood. She was like a delicate piece of sculpture.

"Manny."

That one word, spoken in a sensuous whisper, drove all rational thoughts from his mind. He swore under his breath.

All his good intentions. All his promises to himself. All gone in a rush of need so swift and strong that he was lost.

He swayed into her softness, delicately ringing her lips with his tongue. She made a small noise and put her hands on his chest, burning him through the denim where she touched.

Braced with one hand on the back of the couch and the other fisted in her hair, Manny kissed her. Then deepened the kiss. And kissed her some more. He plunged his tongue deep, intertwined hers with his and pulled hers back into his mouth. She tasted somehow of a home he didn't know, of the earth on the range, of days in the sunshine and of—cookies.

Dizzy and shaking, he lifted his head to search her eyes. "This is all there can be for us, sweetheart. I don't have anything else to give you. The time will come when I'll have to move on. You know that, don't you?"

"I know." Her eyes had turned the same color as the dancing light in the room. Now golden, they contained darkened rays of deepening passion.

"It doesn't matter," she said, and smiled sadly. "I'll have my memories instead of just empty dreams."

Her fingers moved to the buttons on his shirt while his lips found the satiny white skin of her neck. So good.

She tugged at his shirttail, and before he knew it, he was shrugging out of his shirt. The sofa had become awkward and uncomfortable, so he dragged the quilt off the back and placed it on the floor in front of the fire.

The whole operation only took a few seconds, but when he turned back to invite Randi down with him, he sort of expected to find that she'd changed her mind. When he offered his hand though, she took it and settled down on her knees with him. She put her arms around his neck, pressing her breasts close and putting her mouth on his bare shoulder.

She straightened suddenly, a slight frown marring her smooth forehead. "Hold on." She scooted over to a side table and grabbed something.

"Here." She pitched a foil-wrapped packet onto the quilt beside him.

"Determined and prepared. Exactly the qualities I've always found so endearing in a Girl Scout," he said somberly.

He was teasing, trying to lighten the mood and her nerves. But a fleeting look of sorrow touched her eyes and wrenched his heart.

"Oh, baby, I didn't mean anything by that. It's okay. Come here." He pulled her to his chest and kissed away the pout that had formed on her full lips.

Her hands moved to his back, rubbed roughly up and down his spine, came around his waist, slid through the hair on his chest and finally came to rest on his face. Her fingers lightly touched his chin, his brow, his eyelids, finally framing his face as though she was reading him by Braille, learning all the nuances of a man's body.

A roaring, furious need pounded through his bloodstream and threatened to engulf him in flames of desire. He wrapped one arm around her shoulders and one under her bottom, gently laying her on her back—but never breaking the kiss.

He pulled his head back to look at her. Her face was flushed with desire and the warmth of the fire. He drew one ragged breath and lightly skimmed his finger down her neck to the luminescent, pearly colored skin in the vee of her robe.

She raised her eyelids to gaze at him, and he saw that her eyes were aflame—at once both intense and lazily slumberous. He undid her belt and pushed aside the robe, revealing the rich curves of her breasts and the deep-rose-colored nipples, changing tone with the dancing firelight and each breath she took. Oh, what a picture she made. He would keep this vision in his heart for all eternity.

She was a small-boned woman, and both his hands could easily wrap around her rib cage, but when he slid his hands up her sides, her breasts fitted exactly into his palms. He flicked his thumbs across her nipples and heard her gasp. As he took his eyes off her puckering tips to gaze into her face, he found her lips parted and her eyelids heavy.

He couldn't decide what to taste first. She was a fiesta platter full of pleasure just waiting for him to eat his fill. So he leaned down, quickly licked her nipples, then lightly kissed her eyelids. She moaned softly and he felt compelled to move to her parted mouth. He nipped her and slid his tongue between her lips greedily.

She dug her nails into the flesh on his arms, gripping him tightly and sending his manhood into screaming arousal. He heard himself panting hard. All his good intentions of taking things slow disappeared with the animal need that overtook him. He grabbed her wrists with one hand and pulled them over her head.

He shoved one knee between her thighs while he sucked hungrily on her neck, moving quickly to the curve of her breast. She cried out when he returned to feasting on her tender peaks once more. Consumed with an aching hunger, he lost himself again as she arched her hips against his.

Randi heard herself squeal with pleasure and joy as Manny tasted her belly. He ran his mouth over her body like some exquisite instrument of sexual torture, using the flat of his tongue, nipping with his teeth and sucking with his lips. She clutched at his hair, grabbing huge handfuls of the silken strands. They were wild with passion together, and she felt helpless and powerful at the same time.

She reached for the buttons on his jeans, but he undid them himself and had the jeans off before she could move. The light in the room was dim as the fire died back, but she did manage to catch a glimpse of the man naked. It cost her a moment of anxiety, worrying that she'd never be able to accommodate him. But soon he put his mouth on the place that was aching the most for him, sucking through the silk of her panties, and she forgot everything—including how to breathe.

He began tearing at her new lace panties, and she heard them rip as he growled with abandon. Suddenly he paused, reaching out to grab the foil packet. She tried to judge how she was feeling at the moment, but she was so swept up in the euphoria of the sensual explosions creating waves of need within her that she just let go.

Before she could take another breath, he lay over her, leaning up on his elbows to keep from squashing her. Without being told to do so, she opened her thighs and he nestled himself between her legs. The sensation of having him close and warm against her was so poignant and yet so savage at the same time that she became overwhelmed with emotion.

She felt him nudge the opening to her body with his flesh and she gasped. He stilled against her.

"This is it, Randi. Stop me now, if you want to."

"Please don't stop. I'm so thankful you're the one."

He moaned deeply and placed a hand under her buttocks, lifting her hips against him. "Relax, sweetheart. We're going to take this as slow as I can manage. If it gets too painful, let me know."

She consciously registered the tension and controlled need in his voice, until she became totally absorbed in her own body's growing tensions. He entered her slowly, and she was aware of the sensation of size and warmth. He withdrew for a second and eased in again, going a little deeper.

It wasn't painful. In fact, the pleasurable friction was unlike anything she'd ever felt before. It hit her then that this was the ultimate connection between two people. The way to be inside someone else's soul.

# Eleven

"**O**h, Manny," Randi moaned.

Her heart fluttered wildly, and she was thrilled right down to her toes. One or two more movements and she would really be a woman.

"Am I hurting you?" His breathing was labored, but he seemed more in control than she felt.

"No. It's…it's…good so far."

He remained stationary, poised at the barrier to her inner woman. "I can't bear the thought of hurting you," he groaned. "But this *will* hurt. Can you stand it?"

She could stand anything as long as Manny was right here with her. She rubbed her hands down his sides and slipped them around his waist. "I'm ready. Go for it."

When he pushed gently forward, she rose eagerly to meet him. The sharp pain made her cry out.

"Damn." He gazed at her with a troubled look and stilled within her again.

''It's okay,'' she murmured. ''The pain's going away now. Complete me. Love me the way a man is supposed to love a woman.''

Manny was lost. With a groan he pushed deep inside her. He fitted tightly within her glorious heat, and there was nothing but Randi all around him, surrounding him with sensuality.

She writhed and pulsated, sobbing and begging with deep, guttural cries. He grabbed her up and violently thrust into her, deeper and deeper until he began to feel her shudder against him.

They became a team. Together they were transported to the wild heart of the open range, the feral world of intoxicating completeness. He threw his head back and howled, as the earth-shattering climax rocked through her and hit him with a burst of uncontrolled and glittering intensity.

When he could finally catch his breath, he rolled over but kept her welded to him in one possessive move.

The effects of the experience left him shaken and confused. He'd never felt like this before—ever. It seemed like he'd walked through fire, stepped into an animal's skin. She was his mate, his better part. The beast inside him fought to take over her soul, capturing her forever for his own.

He tried to make sense of the sensations. She was supposed to be the one who chased fantasies. He was the one grounded in realism. But every nerve within him was raw and exposed. He suddenly felt as though he was an intricate part of a world he'd never belonged to before—and he didn't like the feeling one bit.

''Sweet mercy,'' she breathed against him.

Randi couldn't be silent any longer. She'd longed to learn what being with a man was all about. But she never thought it would be like this. She'd lost something more than simply her virginity. Yet it felt as if she'd gained something more, as well.

She sought to put her emotions into perspective. What was going on inside her? Could this be what love was all about? Whatever it was, she felt wild and free—and it made her want to weep with joy.

"You all right?" His voice cut through her distraction.

"Better than all right. I feel...it was like soaring in the sky." She knew she was babbling, but she couldn't help herself.

"I think I'd better move. You're going to be sore enough as it is." He let go of her, and she felt chilled.

"No! Please don't go." She flipped over and wound her arms around his neck, plastering herself to his body. "Please hold me. Do you think if we wait a while we can do that again?"

"Hmm. It wouldn't take long if you stay where you are."

"Really? So soon?" Sure enough, she felt his erection pressing against her belly and she snuggled closer to him.

Her books had all been way off when it came to Manny.

"Honey, this is no good." He pulled one of her arms away from his body. "We need to get you into a warm bath and off to bed so you can relax. I want everything to be right."

"It is right. And I don't want a bath. I want you. I love you."

"Dear God." He broke her embrace and rolled over.

He'd been afraid of something like this. He'd lost his

control, and it was Randi who would have to pay the price. He was the lowest of the low.

"But...what's wrong?" she asked quietly. "What did I say?"

"Randi, listen to me for a minute." He wrapped the quilt around her and pulled her up beside him. "I'm not what you need. I'm really one of the bad guys...a creep."

She opened her mouth as if about to interrupt him, but he put a finger to her lips to silence her.

"No, I don't mean a criminal. I soothe my conscience by finding justice for others through Operation Rock-a-Bye. But I'm the kind of man your mother would warn you against if she were here."

He felt he owed her an explanation. Even if it was something he'd never before said aloud.

"I've been a worthless jerk since I was a kid." He'd thought that the nightmare he'd had was a reminder of his failure as a child. Now he knew he'd been wrong.

"When I was about ten my family was working in the fields. They'd left me back at the truck and in charge of my baby sister. She was a toddler, and I was annoyed because she took so much attention. I wanted to be a grown-up and work in the fields, too."

Randi was watching him with a wide-eyed innocence that tore at him. He looked down at his hands.

"I'd let her out of the truck to walk around. She was such a pain in the neck." He had to swallow hard to continue. "A van loaded with local teenagers appeared out of nowhere at that moment. They showed up around the fields occasionally to taunt the farm workers that couldn't speak their language. Called us names and threw rocks."

"No. They didn't..." Randi whimpered.

"They never saw her. I doubt that they ever even realized what they'd done. Her dress caught on their front bumper when they sideswiped her. Dragged her a hundred feet before she was thrown into a ditch."

"Oh, my God." Randi covered her face with her hands.

Manny knew now that his nightmare from the other night wasn't about Ricky or his baby sister. The person he'd been trying to save was Randi. He'd tried to keep her from being destroyed emotionally. To keep her safe from him. And he'd failed. Once more in his life he'd failed someone that mattered.

"But it wasn't your fault," she cried. "You couldn't have stopped them. You were just a kid."

"My whole life has been one miserable screwup after another." He turned his face away from the sight of her tears. "You can't love me. My heart is so full of holes, if you could hold it up to the light, you'd see right through it. I don't know what love means. See me for what I really am. Protect your own heart."

Randi never really knew the meaning of the word *anguish* until Manny had denied her love. She knew he was wrong about himself, but she couldn't find a way to make him understand. If she'd just been a little smarter—or a little more experienced—she'd have convinced him that he hadn't screwed anything up. She loved him no matter what he thought he'd done. And she always would.

But Manny wouldn't let her explain. He'd carried her upstairs and tenderly put her to bed, telling her over and over to forget about him.

Days later he'd still barely spoken to her. When it became clear that he was guilt-ridden about having to hurt her, she quit begging him to listen. Instead, she covered up her pain and decided that the best way to show her love was to let him go.

He'd never really been hers to keep. She was a big girl and should have known better than to fall for a man who'd made it clear from the beginning that he would never stay with her.

She felt like the tin man from that old storybook her mother used to read to her. She knew now, for sure, that she had a heart—because it was breaking.

When she'd been little, her father had given her a lecture on ranching. About how dicey it was to try to make a living off the whims of Mother Nature.

"Life is full of potential pitfalls, little girl," he'd told her. "But if you don't take the risks, you don't gain anything."

She saw now that what he'd said applied to love, as well. If she hadn't taken a chance on Manny, she'd never have known what true love was all about. He'd been more than worth the risk.

Throughout the next week, Randi thought a lot about taking chances and the risks involved with life. She finally came to the conclusion that she'd been emotionally coasting through life. Hiding from the pain of loving someone only to lose them again. She'd started in that direction when she'd lost her beloved father, and the heartbreak of watching her mother deteriorate before her eyes had kept her hidden in life's closet ever since.

Finding love with Manny had opened her eyes. She vowed to never hide from life again. She knew there would never be another lover to compare to Manny, but she decided to take a chance at seeking out new adventures and new relationships.

What did she have to lose? After all, no future loss

could ever be as painful as having Manny—only to lose him.

Today had dawned in typical late-fall fashion. Crisp and clear, the air smelled of the coming winter. It never snowed much here on the Edwards Plateau, but this morning the frost had been particularly heavy. The puddles of rain water had even had a light covering of ice before the sun had melted them.

Randi made up her mind. Today she would change the direction of her life.

For almost a week now Manny had stayed away from the house. He'd come back only rarely to shower and change, to check on Ricky and to tell Randi that he felt he was close to uncovering his suspect.

Soon he and the baby would be gone. She had to be prepared for the loneliness. She had to find a way to go on.

After lunch Randi dressed Ricky in the little sailor suit that Manny had bought him for the wedding. She was surprised that he'd almost grown out of it. Maybe she wouldn't send the outfit off with him when they left her. Maybe she'd just keep it to remember him.

Sighing, she strapped the baby into his car seat in the back of her old reliable Suburban and headed for Lewis Lee and Hannah's place. As she'd imagined, Lewis Lee was off doing chores on the ranch, but Hannah invited her and the baby inside.

"Can you keep Ricky for the afternoon for me, Hannah?" she asked as the older woman poured her a hot cup of tea.

"Sure I can," Hannah grumbled. "But I was hoping for a little visiting time with you, too. What've you got planned?"

"I'm going over to see my stepfather."

"What? After the way he treated you on your wedding night?" Hannah openly stared and shook her head. "You must be crazy. What if he hits you again?"

Randi smiled at her dear old neighbor. "He won't. He was just frustrated that night because I wouldn't give in to his demands. And I think maybe he was a little hurt that I hadn't told him about the wedding. I've forgotten it."

"Don't be foolish, girl. No good can come from seeing him. What do you expect to do there, anyway?"

"I've decided to let him sell off the ranch. We'll need to talk over the terms."

Hannah choked on her last sip of tea, and Randi rushed to pat her on the back. It hit Randi, a little belatedly, that her old friend might be worried about what would happen to her own home.

"Oh, don't worry, Hannah. I'll make sure you and Lewis Lee can live here as long as you like. I intend to have Frank set up a trust for you like Daddy did for Mama. It'll pay you a little to live on and take care of all your medical bills."

"I'm not worried about us, child," Hannah sputtered. "But what about you? What will you do without the ranch?"

"I'm finally going to college…if I can find one that'll have me."

"And where will that leave Manny? And the baby?"

"Uh." She'd forgotten Hannah didn't know that the men in her life would soon be history.

Fortunately, Hannah had lots more questions and didn't wait for her to answer that one. "How can you walk away from your family's heritage? You've sweated blood and tears over this place in order to keep from losing it. Don't you care about the land anymore? Don't you care about your promise?''

Randi could feel her tears backing up like a dammed river, threatening to break over the edge. "Of course, I care. But it's over. The bank won't give me any more credit. There's nothing left to sell off but the land." This was killing her, but it was the only way.

"I never thought I'd live to see the day when a Cullen gave up."

"Sometimes people have to accept reality, Hannah. It's time for me to grow up, make the most of a bad situation and find a new life."

Manny strode into the Willow Springs Public Library and found Marian in her office. Something had been nagging at the back of his mind for days. Every time he'd run into a stone wall in his investigation, he'd had a fleeting sensation that he'd overlooked something important.

It was bad enough that his conscience mocked him night and day for using Randi so badly. He'd managed to wreak havoc with her heart as well as his own. If he also messed up his Operation Rock-a-Bye assignment, he'd never be able to live with himself.

"Got a couple of minutes for a few questions?" he asked.

Marian directed him to sit across from her. "I always have a little time for Randi's husband."

Uh-oh. He would have to be careful about how he worded this. The town librarian was bound to be a fountain of information, but she'd never help him if she thought doing so would hurt her friend. And if he found what he'd been seeking, Randi would face a very public hurt when he took Ricky and left for good.

He was glad he had a plan and a story. He decided to stick to them.

"Randi and I think it would be best if she legally adopts Ricky." At her confused look, he continued. "You've seen her with him, Marian. They belong together. They really love each other. What if something happened to me? Randi might not have a legal right to him."

Marian nodded. "I think I read somewhere about a baby's grandparents getting custody after the death of its mother...even though the stepfather wanted to raise the child as his own. Blood relations seem to have all the legal rights."

She grimaced. "Does Ricky have grandparents like that?"

Without really answering, Manny smiled and continued.

"We're stumped over how to go about it. Adoptions are way out of our league. But I figured you'd know a lot of different things and you're familiar with nearly everyone around these parts. You have any ideas to help us?"

She leaned back in her chair. "Well, I know of someone who might help, but I doubt that you'd be interested."

"Tell me," he urged.

"A local girl came to me when she got into trouble a while back. I'd heard about a lawyer in town who usually handles things like trusts and wills and such, but he also sometimes secretly manages private adoptions for people in need. The girl later told me he took care of everything."

"That sounds like he might be just who we're looking for. Do you think he'd help us?"

"I...doubt it." She shook her head absently.

"Why not?"

"Because the lawyer is Randi's stepfather—Frank."

Of course. Now Manny began to piece together the threads of memory that had eluded him lately. The first night he'd met Randi, she'd mentioned that her stepfather was an attorney from Willow Springs. Reid's backtracking from Del Rio had pointed to the fact that their man must be someone familiar with the law, someone like the sheriff or maybe a politician. It also had to be someone who regularly took trips to Mexico. Why hadn't Manny seen the connection?

He thanked Marian for her help and headed back to the ranch. On the way he contacted Reid by satellite phone.

"Stay close to Randi and the baby," his boss demanded. "We'll close the net around this character, but I don't want to take a chance on him getting wise to us while we finish the investigation." Reid paused. "That slimeball will not have an opportunity to get away."

Manny hung up and stepped down harder on the gas pedal. His skin had begun to crawl, and perspiration appeared on his upper lip. Something in his gut told him things were about to go wrong.

He rolled into Randi's yard and barely brought Lewis Lee's truck to a halt before he jumped out and raced to the house. He took the porch stairs in one leap.

The back door banged shut behind him, and he entered the kitchen to find nothing but eerie silence. "Randi?"

A note was taped to the refrigerator door. He breathed a heavy sigh when he read Randi's words, telling him that she'd taken Ricky to Hannah's.

But as he put the note on the table, Manny felt an

uncontrollable urge to make sure they were okay. To see them—to touch them.

He figured he was being unprofessional and too emotional, still he climbed back in the truck and headed down the road to Lewis Lee's house. He was going to feel like an idiot when he found them both enjoying an innocent visit with the neighbors, but he just couldn't seem to stop before he made a complete fool of himself.

A few minutes later he faced Hannah when she came to her kitchen door. She had Ricky in her arms, and the baby's mouth was outlined with a gooey chocolate ring.

He chuckled and relaxed. Everything was fine.

"I wondered when you'd show up." Hannah's mood seemed exactly opposite of the picture of domestic bliss she'd presented when he'd first seen her.

His warning signals flared once again. "What's wrong? Where's Randi?"

"She's gone to give up on the dream of five generations. And where is her knight in shining armor—the man who was supposed to make her dreams come true?" Hannah shifted the baby and frowned. "Just where is the husband who promised to take care of her through thick and thin, I'd like to know?"

"Hannah, you're not making any sense. I'm right here. Where is Randi?"

"She's gone to make a pact with the devil." She scowled at him, and Ricky began to fidget in her arms. "If Frank Riley hurts that girl again, Manny Sanchez, there won't be anyplace on earth where you'll be able to hide from my wrath. I'll hold you personally responsible for this whole thing."

"Frank? She's gone to see her stepfather?" He was walking backward as he spoke the words. "Can you take care of Ricky for a while longer?"

Before she answered him, he was back in the truck and rolling down the road. He couldn't think, couldn't breathe. This just wasn't possible.

He'd rather be dead than accept the fact that he'd failed her again. Randi had to be okay. She had to be.

He loved her, damn it. He knew that now, even as he knew he would leave her. He was plain no good.

But if Randi was hurt…if anything had happened to her, his own life wouldn't matter anymore. Nothing would make any difference. He'd kill the man who'd harmed her and surrender his worthless hide to the law. That way he'd never again have a chance to fail someone he loved. Never.

# Twelve

"What do you want?" Frank glared at Randi from the threshold of his modern two-story house.

Even though the house had pillars and a circular drive-way, no one would ever mistake it for being old. Randi never had thought the house looked as if it belonged out here on the Texas range—in some fancy Austin suburb maybe—but not out with the sagebrush and mesquite.

She sucked up her nerve and answered her stepfather. "I'm sorry about the other night, Frank. I've thought over your offer and I've decided I *do* want to sell off the bulk of the ranch for development."

Frank's eyes widened, then narrowed as he gaped at her.

"Finally came to your senses, I see." He moved back and showed her inside. "Go on in the office. We'll talk."

As she moved through the front rooms of the house,

Randi noted that things were in terrible disarray. Papers were strewn across nearly every tabletop. Ashtrays overflowed with cigarette butts and ash. A couple of the chair cushions were lopsided and had major stains on the corners.

The whole place seemed way out of character for the man Randi knew as a meticulous housekeeper. Had he gone totally nuts?

When they reached Frank's office, Randi let him move to the chair behind his desk—but he didn't sit down. Nor did he offer her a seat in one of the newspaper-filled chairs placed across from him. They stood edgily eyeing each other.

"So what changed your mind?" he asked.

Her blood curdled at his snake-oil-salesman's gleam and the hoarse, throaty whisper of his voice. He looked years older than the last time she'd seen him. His shoulders slumped, the pouches under his eyes seemed darker, puffier.

"I need the money," she answered simply. No sense in lying to the man at this point.

"You need the money? Or is it that wetback scum you married that needs it?"

The cruel expression in his eyes revolted her, and his words turned her stomach. "My husband's name is Manny and he has nothing to do with this."

"I'll just bet." He snickered. "I'll have to thank him for getting you to see the light. This marriage may turn out better than I'd thought. Good thing the only idiot you could find to marry you is a lowborn, no-good who's out of a job."

She saw it clearly now. The man was evil. She wanted to scream at him, then run away. Unfortunately, as he was always reminding her, he owned half the ranch and she had to be his partner.

"Look," she muttered, "Manny is not out of a job. He's a federal agent and he's working undercover on some big kidnapping case." She wanted Frank to stop harping on Manny's upbringing. "He's not involved with my decision at all."

Frank's lips thinned into a cold smile, but his eyes danced with nervous energy. "Ahh. You've been assisting the FBI. No wonder I've been feeling them closing in."

He drove his fingers through the wispy remnants left on his head. His hair looked as if it hadn't seen a comb in days. "I should have known that your marriage was a sham. You couldn't even get a damn illegal alien to marry you for real."

His words stung her badly enough to make her take a step backward, away from his venom.

"Listen to me, girl." Frank's smile twisted into a sneer. "From now on you will do exactly as I say. You'll sign everything I tell you to, and you'll tell the FBI only what I say is okay. Got that?"

"What? Why should I do that?" She'd felt a bit shaky, but she noticed her voice getting stronger.

"Because if you don't, I'll make sure you're implicated in the baby-selling scheme. Even though none of the business went on around here, no one will believe you didn't know what your partner was involved with."

"Baby selling? You? Oh, my—"

"I'm sure sorry you said that, Frank."

Randi jerked at the sound of Manny's voice and found him standing in the doorway. His face was tight with anger, and the sharp angles of his jaw were carved into stone.

"Manny. Thank God." She nearly wept with relief at seeing him.

"In a few minutes you *will* be sorry, Mexican." Frank moved fast and pulled a gun from his desk drawer. "Now you and the little missus here will have to kill each other in a jealous rage." He waved the gun at Randi and then after she'd gasped, pointed it back at Manny's chest. "Such a shame for newlyweds."

Manny faced her stepfather calmly, but Randi saw him take a casual sidestep in her direction.

"I'm already sorry, Riley," Manny lamented. "Now I'll have to arrest you before we get a chance to complete our investigation. It'll be messy."

Frank sneered. "Just who's got the gun, Agent Wetback?"

Manny kept talking as if Frank had never spoken. "Of course, the paperwork wouldn't be messy if I just drop you where you stand right now. The coroner might have a time finding all the pieces, but…hell, that's his problem."

Randi was shocked at the tough words, and she felt a little woozy. She held out her hand to steady herself. Manny tried to grab her wrist, dragging her behind him.

His movement strangely comforted her. A profound sense of togetherness rushed through Randi. He really cared about her. The thought gave her a strength of spirit she'd only wished about before.

"Don't try it. Stand still." Frank's face was contorted with rage. "I'd rather not kill you here, but if I must…I must."

Manny stilled, but faced Randi. "Don't be afraid, honey. He won't kill us here." He turned back to Frank. "I'm not sure your stepfather has the guts to pull the trigger at all."

Randi quickly stepped in front of Manny before he could stop her. "I can't believe my mother actually married you, Frank." Manny made another grab for her, but she pulled away from him. "You must've used manipulation and intimidation to convince her. She never could have loved you."

Manny had the idea that Randi was trying to take Frank's attention off him. But he didn't want her to do that, damn it. Judging by the complete mess in the house and the wild-eyed look in Frank's eyes, Manny knew they were in trouble. Regardless of what he'd said to Randi, this jerk had gone over the edge and had nothing to lose by killing them both.

All Manny wanted was to get her safely behind him. Give her an opportunity to make a run for it.

Frank waved the gun at Randi once again. "Shut up. Who cares. All women are stupid. I coerced your mother into giving me control over half the ranch, didn't I?"

He laughed and then wiped the back of his free hand over his mouth. "You never even had the sense to see that I was sabotaging the place to make you want to sell. All those acts of vandalism? All me. You were so dumb and naive you really believed it was bad luck."

It took every ounce of Manny's professional instincts not to lunge at the guy. Instead, he saw his chance. He eased farther around Randi and slid a hand behind his back to the hidden waistband holster he'd started wearing again.

"You were the one causing all the trouble? But why?" she demanded of Frank. "I mean, you had to help pay for those things. Why would you do that to something you owned?"

Frank's eyes bulged and he grimaced. "You just don't get it do you? I tricked you. This place is worth multimillions to the developers. If I could've convinced you to sell, I'd have found a way to steal most of the money. You would've ended up with a pittance, but I would have been wealthy. I'd finally be able to get out of that damn baby-selling business. I've always hated it.

"Not that I care about the brats or their families, mind you. I don't. But finding the lowlifes that do the actual kidnappings across the border is a trying ordeal. Those people aren't worth spit. I detest having to deal with them."

"But… but…" Randi raised her hand to her temple as if she was in pain, but took a step toward Frank. "You bastard."

"Oh, good grief." Frank raised the gun and pointed it directly at Randi's head. "You're just too damn stupid to live."

"No!" Manny shoved Randi aside and pulled the trigger on his Glock while Frank's weapon exploded at the same time.

In the background Manny heard Randi scream. Blinded by the brilliant light of the gun's explosion, he felt the sting of pain as a bullet grazed across his forehead. He tried to keep the Glock from dropping out of his hand—right before he collapsed into black oblivion.

Two days, seven sutures, twenty cups of coffee and what seemed like thousands of hours of debriefing later, Manny met Reid in the parking lot of the Uvalde County General Hospital. The sunshine and the cold, winter-clear air were a welcome relief after the smell of antiseptic and the depressing atmosphere of the hospital.

"How's Randi? Where is she now?" Manny snapped at his Operation Rock-a-Bye boss.

He hadn't been allowed to see her since the shooting,

and every minute that went by without her became more agonizing than the last.

"She's fine," Reid explained. "I've told you she wasn't hurt, every one of the gazillion times that you've asked me about her."

Manny's response was abrupt, short and physically impossible.

Reid chuckled at his curse. "And she's at the ranch right now with Ricky...waiting for you to come get him."

Manny's heart throbbed like the pain in his head under the bandage. Today he must tell her goodbye.

"She was really something, wasn't she, Reid?"

"Yeah. Well...at least *she* stayed upright." He jabbed Manny in the ribs and laughed.

Manny narrowed his eyes and grimaced.

"Okay." Reid sighed. "She was spectacular. When you hit the floor after winging Riley, she had the presence of mind to grab your gun, call the sheriff and keep Riley from running while putting pressure on your bleeding head. She saved your sorry ass...as well as the entire operation."

They had reached the rented car that Manny would use to drive himself and Ricky to San Antonio. Weeks of paperwork and consultations with state attorneys loomed ahead of him. He wasn't particularly anxious to turn Ricky over to the INS, either. He'd vowed to work on that little problem in his spare time.

With a heavy heart and a monumental headache, Manny said goodbye to Reid, who would meet him in a few days at the San Antonio field office. Torn by wanting desperately to see Randi—to touch her and to assure himself she was really all right—and by dreading the thought of taking Ricky from her arms forever, Manny slowly made his way down the farm-to-market roads leading back to the ranch.

"You're such a big boy." Randi held Ricky's hand as the toddler took tentative steps across the kitchen floor.

How would she ever manage to live with the loneliness after the baby had gone? It was hard enough on her, not being allowed to see Manny in the hospital. His boss had told her that Manny was too busy with his debriefings for visitors, but not to worry 'cause his head was too hard to break with just any old .38 caliber bullet. Still, she wished she could've seen for herself. Two days seemed like eternity.

Randi took a deep, cleansing breath and picked up the baby, clutching him tightly to her breast.

The back door banged open, and she heard the familiar bootsteps she'd grown to love. She knew she was hearing them for the last time, and a twinge from her heart traveled to her chest and up into her throat. The resulting lump was too great to swallow and threatened to choke her.

"Hey, there." Manny strode into the room and she felt her knees go weak.

He stepped closer, and the musky scent she knew by heart filled her empty soul. She had to bite her bottom lip to keep the tears from rolling down her cheeks.

"You really are okay, aren't you?" he said in a hushed tone. "You didn't get hurt during the shooting?"

She shook her head, but couldn't find any words. Her gaze was drawn to the bandage on his forehead. Then her hand was drawn to it, fingers gently touching the stark white reminder of the bleeding gash she'd tried so hard to close with the edge of her flannel shirt.

He grinned at her, but his eyes stayed solemn, forcing her to keep her own eyes focused on his, not on the wound. He gently took her hand away from his forehead and, turning her palm up, placed a soft kiss there.

The gesture was so sweet, so tender and yet…it made erotic impulses shoot straight to her belly. A turbulent tide of emotions washed across her, leaving her more weak and shaky than ever.

Manny's voice must have been a little shaky as well. He had to clear his throat a couple of times to speak.

"So…have you thought more about going to college, now that you're free?" His words were light, upbeat, but she suspected he'd wrestled with himself to get them said.

"I've decided I'm not going away to school. I'm going to stay right here on the ranch where I belong." At his confused stare, she hastened to add, "I've applied to a correspondence college. I'll be taking courses in ranch management right here at home. Lewis Lee said he'd be glad to help me with the homework while we worked on the land."

Manny looked thoughtful for a minute. "But what about money? It'll take cash to bring the ranch back to profitability."

"Turns out, there's lots of money in a trust my father left to me." Randi chuckled. "Frank had it hidden in some big-city bank. Your boss helped me locate it and found an attorney to help me regain control of my assets."

Randi hadn't realized that Manny still had hold of her hand until he dropped it. The closeness and warmth of his fingers on hers had felt so right, so like they belonged there.

He smiled, and this time the smile reached his eyes.

"I'm glad for you, Randi. I can rest easier about you now."

He held out his arms, and she knew it was time to turn over the baby.

"I'm proud of you, sweetheart," he said to her as she lifted Ricky toward him. "You've come a long way from the timid little girl who rescued a stranger and his baby from a raging, early-fall flood."

Yes, she certainly had come a long way. She'd become a determined, grown-up woman who knew how to take care of herself and the people around her. She'd learned her lessons from the man who was about to leave her behind. Her heart ached with the pain of remembering his gentle tutoring and realizing she'd never know that again.

"Must you go now?" she asked. "I could fix you something to eat first. Maybe it would be better if you stayed one more night and left first thing in the morning."

"Randi." He settled Ricky against his shoulder. "This is hard enough for me...for us. Please let it go. You know I'm no good for you. I'm no good for anybody."

She didn't know any such thing. She wanted to scream at him that he was the best man she'd ever met— the best man she was ever likely to meet. But she knew he wouldn't listen. He'd spent his whole life convincing himself that he had to hide from decent society. That his every action was a foul-up—destined to destroy, not help, others.

She spun around, unable to face the sight of the two people she loved more than life itself as they left her.

"Aren't you going to walk us to the car?" Manny asked in a soft whisper.

"I...can't." She straightened her shoulders and took a deep breath. "Just leave, please."

She was glad she couldn't see his expression. More than glad she was still able to stay on her feet and not collapse in a heap of tears in front of him.

"Will you be all right?" Manny's voice was hoarse with his own emotions.

"I'll be fine."

A couple of minutes later she had an opportunity to test that theory. His car's engine roared to life and then his tires crunched against the gravel as he drove away for good.

In that last moment of farewell, she knew damn well that nothing would ever be fine again.


Lewis Lee snarled at Randi when she dropped the hammer on his foot. For weeks now she'd been behaving like a spoiled child, and she knew it.

Rebuilding the cattle pens in preparation for the calves, due to arrive this week, was not a barrel of laughs, but it certainly wasn't the nastiest job she'd ever done. Yet every little missed nail or incorrectly sawed piece of wood caused her to lose her temper.

All her days dragged into endless monotony, as each morning dawned like each one had the day before and like each one would the day after. Every night after supper, she'd study until she was too tired to see anymore. Then she would wander the house from top to bottom, listening to the echoes of Ricky's tears and laughter. The house also carried the smooth siren song of lovemaking through the chimney and broadcast the sounds, making it impossible for her to sleep.

She loved the solitude—and she despised it.

"You heard anything from Manny lately?" Lewis Lee

asked, as he picked up the hammer. He began to put away the tools.

"From him? Nope. Not a word since he left." Randi hated that her voice sounded so wounded and rough when she spoke of him. "But Marian heard through the grapevine that the FBI gave him some kind of award...for saving Ricky's life. When I talked to Reid a while back, he told me that Manny had been offered a promotion, too."

She picked up her toolbox and she and Lewis Lee headed home for the day. "I guess he's doing just fine."

"If you don't need me anymore today, I think I'll head on along." Lewis Lee climbed in his truck and took off down the road.

As she approached the yard, Randi was surprised to see a sheriff's car sitting next to her back porch. Her heart turned over in her chest with the fleeting worry that the deputy might have come to deliver bad news. For all she knew, Manny's next undercover assignment might be the one to take his life. She couldn't think about a world without him in it—even though he'd never be part of her life again.

Randi's nerves were shot. What could the deputy want?

As she neared the car, the uniformed figure of a deputy emerged from the driver's seat. The deputy was tall and dark-haired. Not like anybody in the department that she remembered.

Before the man slowly turned to face her, she knew—

Randi stared at Manny as he walked around the car toward her. His expression revealed nothing. Unlike the rough and dangerous man she'd first met on that long-ago stormy night, he was the epitome of a lawman. Starched and pressed khaki uniform. Black, spit-polished regulation boots. And the hair. The black, shiny hair she remembered running her fingers through in the most intimate way was cut shorter and brushed into a military style.

Her body tightened at the sight of him. She fought it. Fought every traitorous desire that ran along each nerve ending. Whatever he'd come about, he wasn't back to stay.

"That the uniform you're wearing for a new undercover assignment?" she asked abruptly.

He'd stopped two feet from her. He stood there gazing at her so nonchalantly that she had the urge to scream.

"It's for a new job, yes."

She yanked off her work gloves and shoved them into the back pocket of her jeans. "I heard you got an award and a promotion. Congratulations." Her voice had the same rough sound to it, and she fought that, too.

"They really weren't meant for me, Randi. You're the one who deserved them. You saved both Ricky and me from the flood. And it was you who captured Frank."

Something died inside her. The flame of hope that had flickered with the thought he might have come for her burned out. She hadn't even realized that she'd dared to hope once again. Foolish girl.

"So where is this new assignment and when do you start?" she asked quietly.

He reached out and took her hand in his. "Randi, *querida,* I've been appointed the new deputy sheriff for Uvalde County. Deputy Wade is going to run for the sheriff's job next month when the old sheriff retires."

"What?" She knew she was gaping, but she couldn't help it. "For real? Not undercover?"

He shook his head and grinned at her sheepishly.

"But what about the FBI? Your job?"

"It was high time I came in out of the darkness, *mi amor*. I finally realized that I liked living out in the sunshine with you." He put her hand to his lips and gently kissed it. "After I received that award, the sheriff offered me this job. Said I would make a great addition to the community."

"You'd make a great addition to any community. You're a good man," she said, then stopped breathing, still afraid to hope for what she wanted.

His eyes burned into her soul. "But to be really respectable I need…a family. I need a wife."

Her breath caught audibly, making him grin again.

He bent on one knee, right there in her dusty, dirty yard, and gazed up with such trepidation that her heart went out to him. He was nervous about this. Uncertain.

"Randi, my love, do you know anyone who might want a miserable screwup? Anyone who might be available to marry the new deputy sheriff?"

She knelt down facing him. "Sorry. I don't know anyone who isn't spoken for already," she said solemnly.

He closed his eyes and sighed deeply. "I was afraid you might not still—"

"Be quiet and listen to me, silly," she said quickly. "I was teasing."

His eyes popped open, and she saw the vulnerability in them. She'd have to be a little less glib for a while.

"I'm not free to marry you because I'm already married…to you." Her mouth curved up in a wry grin.

"But the annulment…I signed the papers a month ago. Didn't Reid send them to—"

"I never signed those papers. I couldn't bring myself to be so final about it." She felt herself blushing.

"Besides," she added quickly, "I figured that if you really wanted them signed, you'd have to come get them yourself. It would've been a good excuse to see you one more time.''

Manny reached for her then, grabbing her up and kissing her senseless. She poured herself into the kiss. Melded herself into him. She'd needed this for so long.

He stood, pulled her up beside him, then swung her up in his arms and carried her inside the house. Before he headed up the stairs, he stopped for one more quick kiss.

He pulled his head back, but kept her tightly in his embrace. ''I can't promise you that I'll never make a mistake or never hurt you, Randi. But I swear to you, we'll never hide from life again. I'll do everything in my power to make sure we'll always spend our lives out in the open...secure in the arms of our family and community.''

# Epilogue

Two weeks later Randi found herself in a familiar situation. She rode with Marian toward the Willow Springs Community Church. The days had grown short in this time right before Christmas, and the sharp winds blew the cottonwood leaves into tiny dust devils across the roads. The lengthening shadows of late afternoon cast a slightly melancholy pallor on Randi's grand day.

"This is just so romantic," Marian gushed as she turned into the church's parking lot.

"I wish Manny hadn't insisted on making a big to-do about our second wedding." Randi tugged on her brand-new veil and smoothed the wrinkles from her great-grandmother's dress.

"But you've always wanted a fairy-tale wedding. The first one was sweet…even if it wasn't meant to be real." Marian scowled at her. "But there won't be any mistak-

ing this one for a fake. All Manny's family and friends
and everyone in town will be there to make sure it's
done right this time.''

"I suppose..." Randi felt a bittersweet ache in her
chest.

"You don't sound very happy. You should be," Marian argued. "You've finally gotten everything you ever
wished for."

"No. Not quite everything," she whispered. Ricky,
the one person that she wished could be here, was lost
to her forever.

The last ten days with Manny had been near heaven.
Before he really had to report for work, they'd managed
a pre-second-wedding honeymoon—mostly taking the
form of uninterrupted days and nights in bed. She smiled
to herself at the thought of another wedding night. She
wouldn't need much instruction for this one.

Still, not everything was perfect.

A half hour later, the ceremony was set to begin.
Randi stood with Lewis Lee in the vestibule waiting for
their cue to walk down the aisle. She could hardly wait
for this ceremony to be over. So far she hadn't had one
minute to meet Manny's family. The church was over-
flowing with relatives and kids—the big family she had
always longed to have was only seconds away.

The slightly open door to the church alcove inched
farther open and Manny stuck his head in to peer at her.

"Hi. Got a minute?" he asked sheepishly.

"Get out of here," she squeaked. "You're supposed
to be waiting at the front of the church. The ceremony
will be starting any minute now."

He grinned at her and stepped into the room. "I wanted to tell you that Witt finally made it."

Witt was to be Manny's best man and had been delayed somehow. Reid had been willing to step in, but Manny insisted they hold off as long as possible waiting for his friend.

"Oh, Manny, I'm so glad. I know how much having him here means to you."

"It means more than you know…to both of us." He stood grinning down at her with the sappiest look she'd ever seen on anyone's face. "His wife, Carley, came with him, and they brought along another wedding guest."

"The more the merrier," she murmured. "I can't wait to meet…"

The door behind Manny opened farther, allowing her to see Witt moving into the room. A beautiful woman with long, auburn hair appeared behind him. She was carrying a child—and not just any child.

The baby in her arms was…Ricky.

"Oh, my…" Randi's tears, so close to the surface today, anyway, streamed from her eyes at the sight of the one person who could make this day absolutely perfect.

"Mama…" Ricky screamed when he caught sight of her. He held out his arms and nearly jumped into her waiting embrace.

Randi scooped him up and hugged him tightly to her chest. Manny stepped closer to them and wrapped his arm around her shoulders, giving her the strength to keep from collapsing with joy.

She looked up through her tears at her husband's dear face. "How long can he stay?"

"Forever, *querida*," Manny whispered. "We have a few papers to sign, but essentially he's ours."

"But...how?"

"Uh, if you'll excuse us, we'll be waiting outside." Carley Davidson grabbed her husband's arm and headed toward the door with Lewis Lee also in tow. "The kids at Casa de Valle will sure miss Ricky. He's been a joy, but he clearly needs you as much as you need him. I'm glad things worked out," she murmured as she closed the door behind them.

Alone with the two most important people in the world, Manny looked into the tear-streaked, pale-green eyes of the woman who had become his whole life and felt the familiar thud of his heart. She was more than his life. She'd saved him from an excruciatingly lonely existence and made him realize his life hadn't ended when he was ten.

"Ricky had no family left in Mexico, so I pulled in a few favors from my pals at the INS," he said. "I'll explain it all later. Right now I'm anxious to get this wedding over with so we can start working on a baby brother or sister."

"Babies? You want us to have more children?" Randi's shining eyes gazed up at him over Ricky's curls.

"Lots more. I come from a big family, remember?"

"Oh, Manny, I've always wanted a big family."

He chuckled at her wide-eyed sincerity. She was amazing—able to go from childish innocence to vamp and finally to earth mother. And to think, she was about to legally be joined with him. He vowed forever to be worth the honor.

He tugged them both closer, placed a kiss on her forehead and leaned his cheek against Ricky's sweet-smelling hair. Instead of endless years of miserably hiding in the shadows, they were on the verge of stepping into the light.

Finally together, the desperado and the virgin faced a magical new beginning.

\* \* \* \* \*

*If you liked*

*DESPERADO DAD,*

*you'll love Linda Conrad's*
*next Silhouette Desire novel,*
*SECRETS, LIES…AND PASSION, #1470.*

## presents

## DYNASTIES: THE CONNELLYS

A brand-new miniseries about the Connellys of Chicago,
a wealthy, powerful American family tied by blood to the
royal family of the island kingdom of Altaria.
They're wealthy, powerful and rocked by
scandal, betrayal...and passion!

Look for a whole year of glamorous and
utterly romantic tales in 2002:

*Where love comes alive*™

# Have you ever wanted to participate in a romance reading group?

## Silhouette Special Edition's exciting new book club!

Don't miss

## RYAN'S PLACE
by Sherryl Woods

coming in September

Get your friends or relatives together to engage in lively discussions with the suggested reading group questions provided at the end of the novel. Also, visit www.readersring.com for more reading group information!

*Available at your favorite retail outlet.*

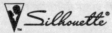

**Where royalty and romance
go hand in hand...**

The series continues in Silhouette Romance
with these unforgettable novels:

**HER ROYAL HUSBAND**
by Cara Colter
on sale July 2002 (SR #1600)

**THE PRINCESS HAS AMNESIA!**
by Patricia Thayer
on sale August 2002 (SR #1606)

**SEARCHING FOR HER PRINCE**
by Karen Rose Smith
on sale September 2002 (SR #1612)

And look for more Crown and Glory stories in
SILHOUETTE DESIRE starting in October 2002!

*Available at your favorite retail outlet.*

# COMING NEXT MONTH

**#1459 RIDE THE THUNDER—Lindsay McKenna**
*Morgan's Mercenaries: Ultimate Rescue*
Lieutenant Nolan Galway didn't believe women belonged in the U.S.
Marines, but then a dangerous mission brought him and former marine pilot
Rhona McGregor together. Though he'd intended to ignore his beautiful copilot,
Nolan soon found himself wanting to surrender to the primitive hunger she
stirred in him....

**#1460 THE SECRET BABY BOND—Cindy Gerard**
*Dynasties: The Connellys*
Tara Connelly Paige was stunned when the husband she had thought dead
suddenly reappeared. Michael Paige was still devastatingly handsome, and
she was shaken by her desire for him—body and soul. He claimed he wanted to
be a real husband to her and a father to the son he hadn't known he had. But
could Tara learn to trust him again?

**#1461 THE SHERIFF & THE AMNESIAC—Ryanne Corey**
As soon as he'd seen her, Sheriff Tyler Cook had known Jenny Kyle was the
soul mate he'd searched for all his life. Her fiery beauty enchanted him, and
when an accident left her with amnesia, he brought her to his home. They soon
succumbed to the attraction smoldering between them, but Tyler wondered what
would happen once Jenny's memory returned....

**#1462 PLAIN JANE MacALLISTER—Joan Elliott Pickart**
*The Baby Bet: The MacAllister Family*
A trip home turned Mark Maxwell's life upside down, for he learned that
Emily MacAllister, the woman he'd always loved, had secretly borne him a
son. Hurt and angry, Mark nonetheless vowed to build a relationship with his
son. But his efforts brought him closer to Emily, and his passionate yearning for
her grew. Could they make peace and have their happily-ever-after?

**#1463 EXPECTING BRAND'S BABY—Emilie Rose**
Because of an inheritance clause, Toni Swenson had to have a baby. She
had a one-night stand with drop-dead-gorgeous cowboy Brand Lander, who
followed her home once he realized she might be carrying his child. When
Brand proposed a marriage of convenience, Toni accepted. And though their
marriage was supposed to be in-name-only, Brand's soul-stirring kisses soon had
Toni wanting the *real* thing....

**#1464 THE TYCOON'S LADY—Katherine Garbera**
*The Bridal Bid*
When lovely Angelica Leone fell into his lap at a bachelorette auction, wealthy
businessman Paul Sterling decided she would make the perfect corporate
girlfriend. They settled on a business arrangement of three dates. But Angelica
turned to flame in Paul's arms, and he found himself in danger—of losing his
heart!

SDCNM0802